# Mrs. Piggle-Wiggle's Farm

# MRS. PIGGLE-WIGGLE'S FARM

## BETTY MacDONALD

*Pictures by* MAURICE SENDAK

HarperCollins*Publishers*

*ISBN 0-397-31713-1*
*ISBN 0-06-440150-2 (pbk.)*
*Library of Congress Catalog Card Number 54-7299*

# CONTENTS

I. THE NOT TRUTHFUL CURE      7

II. THE PET FORGETTER CURE      32

III. THE DESTRUCTIVENESS CURE      53

IV. THE FRAIDY-CAT CURE      76

V. THE CAN'T FIND IT CURE      106

# I. THE NOT TRUTHFUL CURE

MRS. HARROWAY was out in her side yard setting out zinnias. She was very happy. The zinnia plants were not only unusually large with short thick stalks and bright green leaves, but zinnia plants were mighty scarce that year. Mrs. Harroway hummed to herself as she dug holes for the fine young plants. How lucky she had been to get the last flat Mr. Wisner had. How lovely the zinnias were going to look against the freshly painted white house. She filled a hole with water, put in a little fertilizer, set in a plant, pushed earth around it and tamped it down firmly with her trowel. By three-thirty she had planted them all. Standing up and stretching to get the crick out of her back, she called to her neighbor, Mrs. Wintergreen, who was setting out asters in her yard across the hedge, "Oh, Caroline, do come and see my zinnias! They are the finest plants I have ever had."

"Oh, they are beauties," said Caroline Wintergreen coming through the hedge gate. "I can see from here. Where in the world did you get them?"

"From Mr. Wisner," said Mrs. Harroway. "They were the last ones he had."

"Oh, darn," said Mrs. Wintergreen.

"Never mind," said Mrs. Harroway, "I'll bring you

over armloads of zinnias every morning when they are in bloom."

Just then the front gate crashed open and Fetlock Harroway, aged nine, came bellowing into the yard. "Mama," he bawled, "the kids won't play with me."

"And why not?" asked Mrs. Harroway taking a handkerchief out of her sweater pocket and swabbing away his tears.

"I don't know," wailed Fetlock. "They just don't like me. I guess it's because I'm so delicate and wear glasses. Children don't like invalids."

"Nonsense," said Mrs. Wintergreen. "Wembley Rustad wears glasses and has braces on both legs and the children all like him. In fact he's the most popular boy in his cub scout troop. I'm his den mother and I know."

"That's true, Fetlock, darling," Mrs. Harroway said. "Everybody loves Wembley."

"Well, I don't," Fetlock said. "I hate, despise, abominate, loathe and detest him. He called me a liar."

"Oh, no," said Mrs. Harroway in a shocked voice. "Are you sure?"

"You bet I'm sure," Fetlock said. "He just finished right outside our gate."

"That's dreadful," said Mrs. Harroway. "And I don't blame you for being angry but perhaps he'll apologize."

"Why did he call you a liar?" asked Mrs. Wintergreen.

"I don't know," said Fetlock hanging his head and digging a hole in the grass with the toe of his shoe.

"Of course you know," said Mrs. Wintergreen. "Now tell me."

"I won't," said Fetlock. "It's none of your business and I won't tell you."

"Why, Fetlock, darling," said Mrs. Harroway. "Mother doesn't want her boy to be rude. Apologize to Mrs. Wintergreen, son, and then run upstairs and lie down on my chaise longue. You look so tired!"

Fetlock said nothing but continued to dig in the grass until he had a hole big enough for a gopher.

Mrs. Harroway said, "Speak up, sweetheart, tell Mrs. Wintergreen how sorry you are. And hurry, you do look so peaked."

Fetlock said nothing. The hole grew big enough for a badger. Looking down at Fetlock as if he were a beetle, Mrs. Wintergreen said, "Well, Helen, I must get on home if I want to finish setting out those asters before dinner."

Mrs. Harroway said, "Please excuse Fetlock, Caroline, he's just a bundle of nerves." Mrs. Wintergreen banged the hedge gate behind her.

Taking Fetlock's grubby, rather sticky hand in hers, Mrs. Harroway led him up to her room, laid him out, muddy play shoes and all, on her white velvet chaise longue, covered him with her white satin quilt and said, "Now rest, lambie pie."

Closing his eyes behind his spectacles, Fetlock said, "Before I rest, Mumsie, dear, may I have something to eat?"

"Oh, sweetheart, of course," said his mother. "What would you like, some broth?"

9

"No," said Fetlock. "I was thinking more of a chocolate malted milk, a big piece of chocolate cake, some strawberry pop and two or three Giant Size Tutti Frutti Nut Chocolate Bars."

"All that?" asked Mrs. Harroway.

"Yes," sighed Fetlock, "I don't really want it but I must try and keep up my strength."

"What a dear brave little boy you are," said Mrs. Harroway hurrying out of the room.

As soon as he could hear his mother's footsteps on the stairs, Fetlock jumped off the chaise longue, ran over to the bedside table, opened the drawer and took out a box of chocolates. He stuffed four in his mouth and six in his pocket, then went to the window and yelled out at Mrs. Wintergreen who was on her knees by her perennial bed, "Hiya, old busybody!"

Fortunately, his mouth was so full of chocolates it sounded like, "Blug, blug, oh, bluggy."

Mrs. Wintergreen didn't even turn around.

When Mrs. Harroway came staggering in a few minutes later with Fetlock's little snack, he was lying on the chaise longue again, his eyes closed. Mrs. Harroway thought he looked so beautiful she almost cried. Making her voice as gentle as a dove coo, she said, "Did you call, sweetheart?"

"No," said Fetlock, "I was asleep."

"I was sure I heard someone calling," said his mother propping him up with lace pillows and arranging the tray on his bony little knees.

"Perhaps I called out in my sleep," Fetlock said grabbing the chocolate cake and taking a huge bite of the frosting. "I'm very restless, you know."

"You poor child," said Mrs. Harroway. "Would you like Mother to read to you?"

Before Fetlock could answer the telephone rang. Mrs. Harroway hurried out in the hall to answer it on the upstairs extension. She said, "Oh, yes, Mrs. Mallett, yes, yes, yes, are you sure? Are you positive? Fetlock? I'll speak to him. I'm terribly sorry. I can't understand it, are you positive? Yes, I'll speak to him right away."

But when she went in to speak to Fetlock he was gone, as were the malted milk, the chocolate cake and the two Giant Size Tutti Frutti Nut Chocolate Bars.

Sighing Mrs. Harroway brushed some crumbs off the chaise longue.

The telephone rang again. With a worried frown she picked up the receiver and cautiously said hello. Then her face lit up like a Fourth of July sparkler. She chirped happily, "Oh, how sweet of you, Mrs. Workbasket. I'd be simply delighted! Of course, yes, yes, yes, yes, of course. Luncheon tomorrow? Oh, I'll be there. You can count on me."

Hanging up the telephone she rushed to the window and called excitedly to Mrs. Wintergreen. "Oh, Caroline, it's happened! It's happened! Mrs. Workbasket has invited me to join the Earnest Workers. Isn't that wonderful! The first meeting is tomorrow at lunch. Oh, I do hope they will like me! Do you think they will? It would mean so much to Warner's business."

"Of course they will like you," said Mrs. Wintergreen. "There are twenty-five members and they all are intelligent and have children about the ages of ours. Well, I must finish these asters. I'll see you at Freda Workbasket's tomorrow."

In the excitement of being asked to the most exclusive women's club in town Mrs. Harroway forgot all about the call from Mrs. Mallett who had told her that Fetlock had roller skated through her cottage tulips and *she wanted something done about it!*

At dinner that night Fetlock looked pale and was very quiet. Mr. Harroway was worried about the income tax and government waste and so Mrs. Harroway very wisely did not bother them with problems but smiled and smiled and thought about her wonderful new club.

The luncheon the next day should have been an overwhelming success. The table was decorated with pink tulips, a pink tablecloth, pink candles, pink napkins, and pink nut dishes. The main course was a maraschino cherry, walnut, marshmallow, pineapple, strawberry, cream cheese and cabbage molded salad, accompanied by pink biscuits. There were also pink mints and pink gumdrops. And luckiest of all, Mrs. Harroway just happened to be dressed entirely in pink with even pink gloves and pink roses on her hat. All through lunch she was so happy and gay everybody said, "You look adorable, Helen dear, I wish I'd worn pink." Mrs. Workbasket was very proud that she had asked her.

Then the members of the Earnest Workers moved into the living room for the business meeting and that was the end of Mrs. Harroway's happiness. As soon as each lady had found a chair and helped herself to the pink mints and pink gumdrops, Mrs. Feathering stood up and said, "Fellow members of the Earnest Workers, I do not wish to appear snobbish or unkind but before voting on our new member I feel that I must ask a few questions. Mrs. Harroway, is it true that your husband is a burglar who is known the world over for his clever jewel robberies?"

Mrs. Harroway's face turned scarlet and she swallowed her pink gumdrop whole. She said, "Fanchon Feathering, how dare you say a thing like that about

Warner? You know perfectly well, that he is the Executive Vice-President of Rocko Cement."

"Well," said Mrs. Feathering, "my information came straight from the lips of Warner's own little boy. Last week he was over playing Canasta with Winifred and he told Vernon and me that his mother and daddy could never go out any place because his daddy was hiding from the London police and the Paris police and the Russian police and the FBI. He also told us that Warner's picture was in every post office in Europe and that he is training Fetlock, I believe that is your son's name, to work with him. He said that so far all his father would allow him to steal were the little things like rings and watches but he thought he would be ready for the big stuff by Christmas."

Mrs. Gorman jumped up and said, "But Fetlock told us that his father was a train robber."

Mrs. Roberts said, "He told me his father was a confidence man who robbed widows. He warned me never to pay attention to him when he talked about investments."

Mrs. Harrison said, "He told Aunt Elsie and me that Mr. Harroway was a cowboy who had hurt his back breaking wild horses. Fetlock said he was a cowboy too until he was kicked in the forehead by a steer. The blow affected his eyesight, which is why he has to wear glasses. Really, Mrs. Harroway, I don't like to interfere, but I do think it is nothing short of cruel to allow such a small child to bulldog steers."

Before Fetlock's mother could answer, Mrs. Pinwheel said, "But none of that could be true, because only yesterday Fetlock told me all about his lonely childhood and how he had to sell papers and work in a factory to make enough money to buy medicine for you when you were sick, Helen, and while Mr. Harroway was in the penitentiary for making counterfeit money."

Mrs. Gurch who had seven children shrieked, "Counterfeit money! That's not what he told me. He said that his father sold little children. He said that he gathered them up at playfields and sold them to orphanages."

Mrs. Harroway, her face as white as paper, said, "Not one word of this is true. My husband is a fine upright honorable citizen. Fetlock is a dear, sensitive, loyal little boy. I'm sorry I ever came to your old club. I never did want to be a member anyway!" She began to cry.

Mrs. Mallett said, "Before you go, Mrs. Harroway, I wish you would tell me what you intend to do about my tulips." She turned to the other women. "Yesterday Fetlock deliberately roller skated through my cottage tulips and crushed and injured seventeen. Obviously his mother doesn't care."

Mrs. Harroway said, "I do care. I care terribly about your tulips, Mrs. Mallett, but I was so excited when Mrs. Workbasket called me that I forgot. What would you like me to do, pay you for them?"

"Oh, heavens, no," said Mrs. Mallett. "I wouldn't dream of anything like that. I didn't intend to make any trouble, I just thought you should know. I think a normal mother wants to know when her child performs vandalous acts. I know I would. I would want to know anything like that a child of mine did, although goodness knows, Williver is really too good. Too good to live, his old Irish nurse used to say. Naturally I didn't expect you to pay for my tulips. How could you. They were very very rare and in full bloom. Really priceless. However, if you insist, I might accept some other plants. Zinnias perhaps. I noticed on the way over here that you had some fine young plants."

"Oh, I have," said Mrs. Harroway. "They are strong and stocky and very healthy. I'll bring them over to you as soon as I get home."

"Oh, there is no hurry," said Mrs. Mallett. "But I would like to get them set out before dark. Of course zinnias aren't as pretty as cottage tulips but I guess I can't be particular, can I?"

Mrs. Harroway blew her nose on her pink handkerchief, gathered up her pink gloves and purse and went into the bedroom for her pink coat. Her happy day was spoiled and she wanted to die. Big tears made polka dots down the front of her pink suit and splashed on to her purse. Then Mrs. Workbasket, who had invited her to the Earnest Workers Club in the first place, came into the bedroom. Putting her arm around Mrs. Harroway she said, "Don't pay any attention to that hateful Crystal Mallett, Helen dear. Her little Williver rode his bicycle all over my azaleas last year and she not only didn't replace them, and didn't pay for them, but she wouldn't apologize and she wouldn't send Williver to Mrs. Piggle-Wiggle."

"Mrs. who?" asked Mrs. Harroway sniffing.

"Mrs. Piggle-Wiggle," said Mrs. Workbasket. "She is a dear little woman who adores children and knows just how to handle them. Really she has cured almost every child in this town of faults."

"But how does she cure them?" asked Mrs. Harroway beginning to cry again as visions of Fetlock locked in a dark cellar and being beaten with chains floated in front of her eyes.

"Oh, she has many ways," said Mrs. Workbasket. "Some magic and some not. But I'll tell you this, Helen, every single child in this town adores her and she has cured most of them of faults. Actually the ones she has cured love her the most of all."

"Well," said Mrs. Harroway blowing her nose, "I'm pretty sure that Fetlock really did tell those stories. He has a fine imagination and he is very lonely because none of the children will play with him. Where does this Mrs. Piggle-Wiggle live?"

"She used to live here in town in a funny little upside down house," said Mrs. Workbasket, "but last winter she bought a small farm just at the outskirts of town in Little Spring Valley. She has a nice white farmhouse, a large red barn with a big hayloft, a cow and a calf, a horse, some pigs, chickens, turkeys, geese, sheep, a cat and a dog. I believe she even has a parrot and a hive of bees. Since she moved to the farm she usually invites the children to come out and stay with her until they are cured. She says this is a big relief to the parents, fun for the children and makes life very interesting for her animals who are always anxious to help with her work."

"Are you sure it would be safe for Fetlock?" asked Mrs. Harroway anxiously. "He is so delicate and high strung."

"Actually Fetlock would be much safer at Mrs. Piggle-Wiggle's farm than he would be here in the city," Mrs. Workbasket said. "And he might gain a little weight. He looks awfully puny for his age."

"It's his tremendous brain," said his mother. "His brain is so huge it takes all the nourishment from his little body."

"Be that as it may," said Mrs. Workbasket drily, "I think a stay with Mrs. Piggle-Wiggle would be the best thing in the world for him. I think she could even cope with his tremendous brain. Why don't you call her right now? Here is her telephone number."

And so Friday afternoon just as Mrs. Piggle-Wiggle was taking a pan of blackberry tarts out of the oven, a large green car turned into her farm.

"Oh, how nice," she said to Lightfoot, her cat. "Fetlock Harroway will be here for supper."

From all the stories she had heard about Fetlock Mrs. Piggle-Wiggle rather expected to see a great big red-faced swaggering bully come bursting out of the car. Instead Mr. Harroway, with a great deal of difficulty and accompanied by piercing shrieks and anguished howls, pulled out from the back of the car a skinny pale little boy wearing horn rimmed spectacles. As he lifted him out the little boy's macaroni legs and arms flailed the air wildly and in one last convulsive effort he grabbed the doorhandle and hung on shrieking, "Kill me! Shoot me! Cut my veins but don't leave me, Daddy!"

Gathering the arms and legs into a bunch like flowers, Mr. Harroway detached Fetlock's fingers from the door handle, carried him over and dumped him in the grass by Mrs. Piggle-Wiggle's back porch. Then turning to Mrs. Piggle-Wiggle, who had come out on the porch to watch the proceedings, he said, "The boy doesn't seem too enthusiastic about staying. Do you think I'd better take him back home?"

"Certainly not," said Mrs. Piggle-Wiggle leaning over and brushing some of the dusty sneaker marks off Mr. Harroway's blue business suit. "You just leave Fetlock here with me and he'll be fine. However, if I were you I wouldn't tell his mother how he is acting. It might worry her."

"Oh, I won't," said Mr. Harroway opening the door of his car.

Seeing that his father was about to leave, Fetlock who had been floundering around on the grass like a freshly caught trout, jumped to his feet and ran yelping after him.

Immediately Wag, Mrs. Piggle-Wiggle's dog, grabbed the back of his jacket and jerked. Fetlock sat down hard on the grass. He got up again. Wag pulled him down. He got up. Wag pulled him down. He got up. Wag, exasperated, jerked him down and sat on his lap.

"Daddy, Daddy, this ole dog's biting me," Fetlock howled. "Help, help, he's killing me!"

"Pay no attention, Mr. Harroway," Mrs. Piggle-Wiggle said. "Wag is the gentlest dog alive. Just drive away quickly."

Mr. Harroway did and when he got home and Mrs. Harroway rushed out to the car and said, "How was Mrs. Piggle-Wiggle? Did Fetlock like her? Is my dear little boy happy? Did he want to stay?" Mr. Harroway said, "Oh, Fetlock was keen about Mrs. Piggle-Wiggle. He just loves it out there. You've never seen anyone so happy."

"Thank goodness!" said Mrs. Harroway wiping tears out of her eyes.

As soon as his father's car had rounded the bend at the bottom of Mrs. Piggle-Wiggle's lane, Fetlock stopped screaming. As soon as he stopped screaming Wag got off his lap.

Mrs. Piggle-Wiggle said, "My dog's name is Wag. He's very smart."

Fetlock said, "He bit me. Right to the bone. I'll probably get hydrophobia and die."

"Show me the bite," said Mrs. Piggle-Wiggle.

"Oh it doesn't show," Fetlock said. "You see I have a kind of peculiar skin that heals instantly. There's nobody else in the world that has it and the doctors wanted to put me on exhibition."

"Really?" said Mrs. Piggle-Wiggle.

"Yeah, cross my heart," said Fetlock.

"Ha, ha, ha, ha," said Wag.

"Hey, lookit, the dog's laughing," Fetlock said.

"Of course he is," said Mrs. Piggle-Wiggle. "He thinks your story is perfectly ridiculous. Now let's go

in and unpack your things. Did you bring any jeans?"

"Just my cowboy pants," said Fetlock. "You know I used to be a real cowboy in Montana. Used to rope steers and ride in the roundups and everything. I'll wear those pants."

"That's a good idea," said Mrs. Piggle-Wiggle. "Wear your cowboy pants and then you can ride Trotsky out and round up Arbutus."

"Who's Trotsky?" said Fetlock.

"My horse," said Mrs. Piggle-Wiggle. "He's pretty slow but perhaps a regular cowboy like you can make him gallop and buck."

"Oh, I can't ride," said Fetlock.

"But I thought you said you were a cowboy," said Mrs. Piggle-Wiggle.

"I am," said Fetlock, "but I hurt my back bulldogging a steer and so I can't ride any more."

"That's too bad," said Mrs. Piggle-Wiggle. "Trotsky will be very disappointed. I told him that a very nice little boy was going to visit me and he promised to teach you to ride. Of course then, I didn't know that you were a cowboy."

Fetlock said nothing.

Mrs. Piggle-Wiggle took him upstairs, showed him his room and told him to change his clothes. She said, "When you are dressed come down to the barn. I'll be milking."

"Milking?" said Fetlock. "You mean milking a cow?"

"Certainly," said Mrs. Piggle-Wiggle. "I milk Arbutus every morning and every evening."

"Can I watch?" asked Fetlock.

"Of course," said Mrs. Piggle-Wiggle. "That's why I asked you down to the barn."

" 'Course I already know how to milk," said Fetlock. "I worked on a dairy ranch once. It was a great big ranch. In fact, it was the biggest dairy ranch in the whole world. They had ten thousand cows."

"Really?" said Mrs. Piggle-Wiggle.

"Yeah," said Fetlock. "I used to milk five hundred cows a day. Boy, I was a good milker!"

"You must have been," said Mrs. Piggle-Wiggle. "Perhaps you would like to milk Arbutus?"

"Oh, no," said Fetlock, "I had enough milking cows to last me the rest of my life."

"Well," said Mrs. Piggle-Wiggle, "hurry and change and I'll see you at Arbutus' stall."

Mrs. Piggle-Wiggle had fed Arbutus and Heather, the calf, and had the bucket half full of milk before Fetlock finally came clanking in, wearing a complete cowboy outfit, even to spurs, a lasso and two guns.

"Well, my goodness," Mrs. Piggle-Wiggle said, "you really are a cowboy!"

"Sure," said Fetlock, "I told you I was. Watch me, I'll lasso the cow."

"Oh, don't do that," Mrs. Piggle-Wiggle said quickly, "Arbutus might kick over the milk bucket. Are you sure you wouldn't like to milk, I'm getting awfully tired?"

"Well," said Fetlock, "it's been an awful long time since I milked, and I might have forgotten how."

"Oh, that's all right," said Mrs. Piggle-Wiggle. "I'll show you. The first thing is to wash your hands in the milk room."

Fetlock clanked off and Arbutus turned around and winked at Mrs. Piggle-Wiggle.

When Fetlock came back Mrs. Piggle-Wiggle had him sit on the milking stool and she showed him how to milk. At first his hands shook and he was obviously so scared Arbutus wouldn't give down any milk. Finally, however, he caught on and pretty soon the milk was plinking into the bucket. It was unfortunate that just at this point, Arbutus dipped her tail into the bucket and

23

switched it dripping milk into Fetlock's eyes. With a shriek he fell off the milking stool and kicked over the bucket of milk. Mrs. Piggle-Wiggle said, "Arbutus, aren't you ashamed of yourself? Just when Fetlock was remembering how to milk."

Fetlock stood up, wiped some of the milk off his face with his bandana and said, "Gosh, I'm sorry about the milk, Mrs. Piggle-Wiggle."

Mrs. Piggle-Wiggle said, "Don't give it a thought. She has done that to me several times. Here you sit down and finish up and I'll hold her tail."

Fetlock sat down again and pretty soon he had almost a quarter of a bucket of milk.

Mrs. Piggle-Wiggle said, "If you hadn't told me about milking all those hundreds of cows, I would say that you are without a doubt the fastest learner I've ever had on my farm."

Fetlock said, "Well, uh, well uh, as a matter of fact, I really never did milk before. I just wished I could so much I kind of thought I really had."

"Of course," said Mrs. Piggle-Wiggle. "Lots of times I wish I could do a thing so much I think I have done it. That's human nature. However, you are a very, very good milker and I'm proud of you. Now while I strain and cool the milk, you go up in the loft and pitch down some hay for Trotsky."

Fetlock had quite a little trouble climbing the ladder to the loft in his cowboy boots, chaps, holster and spurs, but by using his hands he finally managed. The loft smelled deliciously of hay and dust and from its open hay door, Fetlock could see the farmhouse, the orchard, the hayfields, the pastures, the next farm, even the smokestack of the Rocko Cement plant where his father was Executive Vice-President.

Seeing the smokestack of his father's plant made Fetlock feel queer. Sort of like he'd swallowed a stone. He gulped several times and wished that he were home eating dinner with his mother and father. He was just starting to get tears in his eyes when he heard a funny snorting noise down below him in the barn. He bent over and peered down a little chute above the noise. A large cream-colored horse with a red mane looked up at him and snorted again.

Mrs. Piggle-Wiggle called out, "Trotsky is telling

you he wants his hay, Fetlock. The pitchfork is over by the door."

Fetlock straightened up and started toward the door. His cowboy boots were new and slippery and he fell down twice but he got the pitchfork. He had thrown down about four forkfuls of hay when his feet slipped out from under him and he dropped the pitchfork which was fortunate because the next thing he knew he was lying on his back in Trotsky's manger.

"Oh, my goodness, are you hurt?" called Mrs. Piggle-Wiggle hurrying out of the milk room.

"I don't think so," said Fetlock taking some hay out of his mouth.

"What happened?" asked Mrs. Piggle-Wiggle helping him out of the manger.

"Oh, these old cowboy boots are so slippery," Fetlock said. "You see, Mrs. Piggle-Wiggle, I might as well tell you, I wasn't a cowboy at all, I don't even know how to ride, and my mom only got me this cowboy stuff yesterday."

"Well, that's just splendid," said Mrs. Piggle-Wiggle, "because now Trotsky won't be disappointed. You see he's been just counting on teaching you to ride. As long as you have on your cowboy suit what would you say to a ride up and down the lane after supper?"

"Oh, boy!" said Fetlock.

Trotsky reached down and nuzzled him on the gun holster.

Mrs. Piggle-Wiggle said, "He wants sugar. Here." Reaching in her apron pocket she took out four lumps of sugar and handed them to Fetlock. He put the sugar on the palm of his hand and Trotsky delicately lifted it off, lump by lump with his lips.

"Gosh, he's a sweet horse," Fetlock said beaming up at Mrs. Piggle-Wiggle.

"He is," said Mrs. Piggle-Wiggle. "Just as long as you don't laugh at him. If you laugh at him he'll bite you. It's his only weakness."

"Don't worry, Trotsky, old boy," Fetlock said. "I'll never laugh at you. Never! Because I know how you feel. Sometimes I used to bite people who laughed at me."

Mrs. Piggle-Wiggle said, "Now I want you to meet Lester, my working pig, and Fanny, the mother pig.

Then you can help me feed Heather the calf, the chickens, the ducks, the geese and the mother hens."

From the barnyard a voice shrieked, "What about me? What about Penelope, Mrs. Piggle-Wiggle?"

"Oh, yes," Mrs. Piggle-Wiggle said, "that's Penelope the parrot. She also helps me with my work and when she isn't teasing the animals she is a very nice bird."

"Oh yeah?" shrieked Penelope. "Oh, yeah? Who does most of the work around here anyway? Me that's who. Me, that's who. Me, that's who."

"Stop feeling sorry for yourself and go on up to the house," said Mrs. Piggle-Wiggle.

"I want to see the parrot, where is she?" said Fetlock excitedly.

"She's out in the willow tree by the watering trough."

Fetlock ran to the barn door just as a large green parrot plummeted to the ground out of the willow tree. "Hi, parrot," Fetlock called.

"Hi, yourself," said Penelope crossly. "You mind your business and I'll mind mine."

"Polly want a cracker?" Fetlock called.

"Don't be ridiculous," Penelope said waddling up toward the farmhouse.

"My, but that parrot's crabby," Fetlock told Mrs. Piggle-Wiggle.

"She is," Mrs. Piggle-Wiggle said. "But that very fact is what makes her so useful in curing children of answering back, arguing or being rude."

"Will she ever be friendly to me?" Fetlock asked anxiously.

"Of course she will," Mrs. Piggle-Wiggle said. "I'll let you give her her supper and she'll be your friend in five minutes. Oh, my, it's getting late. Would you gather the eggs for me while I feed the chickens?"

"Sure I will," said Fetlock.

"Do you know how?" asked Mrs. Piggle-Wiggle.

"Oh, yeah, I used to—uh, used to uh—well—no," Fetlock said. "How do you do it?"

Putting her arm around him and giving him a hug, Mrs. Piggle-Wiggle said, "You know, Fetlock, I think we're going to be very very good friends. Now go in the milk room and get the egg basket. It is that funny looking wire basket."

Fetlock stayed with Mrs. Piggle-Wiggle for a whole month. At the end of that time he could ride Trotsky bareback at a full gallop, he could climb any tree in the orchard, he could milk better than Mrs. Piggle-Wiggle, he had gained fifteen pounds, he only wore his glasses when he was reading, he could throw a ball almost down to the end of the lane, he and Penelope were best friends and Wag and Lightfoot slept on his bed.

He was terribly sad at the thought of going home until Mrs. Piggle-Wiggle told him that Mrs. Wintergreen had asked him to be in her Cub Scout troop. "Are you sure, Mrs. Piggle-Wiggle?" he said when she told him.

"Of course I'm sure," she said. "She called me when you were gathering the eggs last night." Mrs. Piggle-Wiggle had really called Mrs. Wintergreen, who was not very enthusiastic until Mrs. Piggle-Wiggle told her how splendidly Fetlock had turned out.

"I mean are you really positive?" Fetlock asked.

"Of course I am, but why are you worried? Why wouldn't they want you in the Cub Scout troop?"

"Well," said Fetlock twisting his right ear. "A long time ago, I mean before I came out here, I used to be an awful big liar. I mean I told the kids all kinds of stuff like my dad was a pitcher for the New York Yankees, I used to be a cowboy, my dad was a international jewel thief, my mom was a movie star—all kinds of stuff. And of course the kids didn't believe me and made fun of me and so I used to kick and bite them and they hated me."

"Well, you aren't the first child who has done that," said Mrs. Piggle-Wiggle calmly peeling apples for a pie.

"You mean," said Fetlock, "that other kids have made up stuff like that too?"

"Of course," said Mrs. Piggle-Wiggle. "It's the most natural thing in the world. You were small and puny. You weren't very good at games. You had to wear glasses. So you just pretended. Of course, now that you're so big and strong, can throw a ball clear to the end of the lane and can ride horseback, you don't have to pretend."

"I know it," said Fetlock. "And the funny thing is that I don't hate the kids any more. When I think of them I like them and I bet they'll like me."

"I bet they will too," Mrs. Piggle-Wiggle said.

The day the Harroways were to get Fetlock, Mrs. Piggle-Wiggle asked them to supper but told them to come early.

They did, they came about four o'clock and when their car turned into the lane, a big tanned husky smiling boy came galloping on a horse to meet them. At first Mrs. Harroway didn't recognize Fetlock at all, but when she was sure it was her son, she was so happy she cried. She said, "Oh, I'm so glad the next meeting of the Earnest Workers is going to be at my house, I want *everybody* to see Fetlock."

Mr. Harroway was terribly proud of his son, especially when he saw him milk. "Well, my golly," he said. "My golly!" Putting his arm around Fetlock he said, "How would you like me to get season tickets to the baseball game for you and me?"

"Oh, boy," said Fetlock.

Just then, of course, Arbutus dipped her tail in the milk and switched it in Fetlock's face. His father jumped about three feet. Fetlock didn't even flinch. Casually wiping his eyes on his sleeve, he said, "Say Dad, hold Arbutus' tail for me, will you? Don't be afraid. She won't hurt you."

## II. THE PET FORGETTER CURE

REBECCA ROLFE loved pets so much her bedroom looked like a zoo. On the bureau was a goldfish bowl with four goldfish in it. On the bedside table was a dish filled with rocks under which lived two turtles. In a can on the desk were twenty-seven tadpoles. In the planter lamp on the desk lived a chameleon. On Rebecca's pillow lay a large gray cat. Under the bed was a basket with four kittens in it. Also under the bed was an English setter who snored. On the foot of the bed slept a Scottie.

Then in the back yard Rebecca had two guinea pigs, a Belgian hare, a baby robin, four white mice, and a bantam rooster.

Her mother and father were glad that Rebecca loved animals except for one thing. Her animals were so noisy. Starting at the crack of dawn every morning the bantam rooster crowed, the dogs skidded down the front stairs after the paper boy yelping, "Let us at him." The gray cat meowed and leapt on Mr. Rolfe's chest and switched her tail in his mouth to let him know she wanted to go out. The guinea pigs squealed. The gold fish splashed. The baby robin shrieked. The rabbits thumped and the white mice squeaked. And every morning Mr. Rolfe stormed out of bed and stamped around shouting, "We've just got to clean out this place.

It's driving me insane. I never get a night's sleep. A man's home should be his castle. A place to relax and find peace. This house is a nightmare. All night long things yelp or crow or squeak or meow or thump or bark!"

Then Rebecca would come out of her room bawling, "If my pets go, I go. We'll all run away."

Mrs. Rolfe would say, "Now, Wolverton, don't be harsh. Don't shout. You are upsetting Rebecca."

"WHO IS SHOUTING?" Mr. Rolfe would roar.

And another day would be spoiled and even if Mrs. Rolfe had buckwheat cakes and sausage nobody would eat any breakfast.

This unpleasant state of affairs went on and on until Mrs. Rolfe was as white as her icebox, Mr. Rolfe was as red and crabby as a crab, Rebecca's face and eyes were so blotchy and swollen from crying everybody thought she had permanent measles.

And the neighbors had begun to complain about the noise.

Then one morning Mrs. Rolfe was talking to her neighbor Mrs. Bent-Smith. Mrs. Bent-Smith said, "My goodness, we're getting crowded over here. Ronald brought Cedric home another pet last night. A snowy owl."

"Does Cedric have pets too?" Mrs. Rolfe asked.

"Oh, my yes," Mrs. Bent-Smith said. "He has seven cats, eleven kittens, six dogs, a parrot, two canaries, a skunk—deodorized of course—a burro, a guinea hen, a mallard duck, a large turtle and thirty-seven goldfish."

"But they're so quiet!" Mrs. Rolfe said. "We have pets too and they bark and yelp and meow and squeak and crow and thump and splash from morning till night. Wolverton is at the end of his patience and I'm afraid Rebecca's face will be scarred from bawling so much."

"I can't understand the animals being so noisy," said Mrs. Bent-Smith. "There must be something wrong. When do you feed them?"

"I really don't know," said Mrs. Rolfe. "Rebecca tends to that."

"Maybe that is your trouble," said Mrs. Bent-Smith. "Perhaps Rebecca forgets to feed and water them. It is a common childish fault—I know, I have to keep after Cedric all the time. Well I must go in, I am baking dog biscuits and I don't want them to burn."

When Rebecca came home for lunch Mrs. Rolfe said, "Rebecca dear, did you feed your animals last night?"

"Oh, gosh, I forgot," Rebecca said.

"Did you feed them this morning?" her mother asked.

"Oh, gosh, I forgot," Rebecca said.

"What about water?" her mother said. "I noticed yesterday that the goldfish needed their water changed and the turtles were almost out of it."

"Oh, gosh, I forgot," Rebecca said through a mouthful of pickle and peanut butter.

"All right, young lady," said Mrs. Rolfe. "You get up from the table this instant and take care of your animals. No, leave your sandwich. You couldn't possibly be as hungry as your pets."

So Rebecca fed and watered her animals and the next day everything was peaceful and Mr. Rolfe had kippered herring and scrambled eggs for breakfast and was as cheerful as the baby robin.

"What a glorious morning," he said passing his cup for more coffee. "I think I'll come home early and cut the lawn."

"You *must* have had a good sleep," Mrs. Rolfe said. "I'll have the lawnmower sharpened."

"Oh, don't bother until I see if I can get off," said Mr. Rolfe quickly. "Where's Rebecca?"

"Out feeding her animals," said her mother. "She has become very conscientious about them which is why they are behaving so nicely."

"Good, good," said Mr. Rolfe. "You see, my dear, shouting at her did some good after all. The trouble with you women is that you always resent any form of discipline for your children. Discipline my dear, makes men great. Show me a man who has had firm discipline and I'll show you a great man. Now when I was a boy . . ."

"You're going to be late for work," Mrs. Rolfe said hastily. "Here I'll get your coat."

Rebecca didn't come in for breakfast and didn't come in for breakfast and didn't come in for breakfast. Mrs. Rolfe heated up the scrambled eggs until they were like rubber and kept the toast hot until it was hard as iron. Rebecca didn't appear until almost twelve o'clock. When she did come in she had green paint in her hair and on one cheek.

"Where in the world have you been?" Mrs. Rolfe said. "I kept your breakfast hot until after eleven."

"I've been over helping Mr. Matthews paint his garage," Rebecca said going to the cookie jar.

"No cookies until after lunch," said her mother. "Did you feed and water the animals before you left?"

"Oh, gosh, I forgot," Rebecca said sitting down at the table and beginning to gulp her soup.

"All right, march right out and take care of them," Mrs. Rolfe said.

"But Mom, I'm starving," Rebecca said. "I didn't even have any breakfast."

"Neither did your pets," said her mother. "Now march!"

And that is the way it went day after day. Sometimes

Rebecca remembered her pets. But more often she didn't.

At her bridge club Mrs. Rolfe was so nervous and upset she couldn't even eat although Mrs. Ellingshall had her favorite ripe olive, cashew nut, raisin, candied cherry, whipped cream and cucumber salad.

Mrs. Ellingshall who had gone to a lot of trouble with the lunch said, "What in the world is the matter with you, Cassandra? You haven't touched a thing. Here have one of these peanut butter sardine and marmalade sandwiches. They are your favorites."

"No thank you, Emily," said Mrs. Rolfe listlessly. "I'm just not hungry."

"Are you sick?" asked Mrs. Foghorn.

"Oh, no," said Mrs. Rolfe.

"Are you and Wolverton having trouble?" asked Mrs. Sharpe.

"Oh, heavens, no," said Mrs. Rolfe. "Of course, not even the Secretary of the United States Treasury could keep a budget the way Wolverton wants it but we get along. Especially as long as I give in to him."

"You poor thing," said Mrs. Mousetrap. "Although I don't know why I say poor thing to you when I have to put up with Evinrude day after day."

"What is the trouble, Cassandra?" asked Mrs. Ellingshall. "You can tell us. We're your best friends and you know we'll never breathe a word of it."

"Well," said Mrs. Rolfe. "It's Rebecca. She has about ten million pets and she forgets to feed them and they squeak and bark and yelp and meow and thump and splash and keep us awake all night. I've yelled at her until I'm hoarse and still she forgets. I'm just at my wit's end."

"The thing for you to do," said Mrs. Ellingshall, "is to call Mrs. Piggle-Wiggle."

"But I thought she had moved out of town," said Mrs. Rolfe.

"She has," said Mrs. Ellingshall. "She moved to a farm, but it is only a little way out and anyway she usually has the children stay with her until they are cured."

"Why don't you go and call her right now?" said Mrs. Mousetrap.

"Yes, call her right now," said Mrs. Ellingshall, "and then you will feel like eating some of my delicious dessert. I made a chocolate, walnut, whipped cream, banana, devils food, cocoanut, peanut brittle frozen custard."

"Oh, yummy," said all the women.

Mrs. Rolfe left the table to call Mrs. Piggle-Wiggle.

"Why, Rebecca Rolfe!" said Mrs. Piggle-Wiggle on Friday afternoon. "You've grown so big I hardly recognized you. And you're very pretty."

"I'm still a tomboy, though," said Rebecca. "I'm the pitcher for the neighborhood baseball team, I was tackle on our football team, and I can spit through my front teeth."

"Good for you," said Mrs. Piggle-Wiggle. "How would you like to learn to milk a cow?"

"I'd love to," said Rebecca. "And I like to pitch hay and clean out the barn and curry the horse."

"Well," said Mrs. Rolfe. "It seems to me that Rebecca will be very happy here."

"How long can I stay?" asked Rebecca.

"How about two weeks?" said Mrs. Piggle-Wiggle.

"Oh, boy, can I, Mom?" asked Rebecca.

"It is 'May I, Mother?' " said Mrs. Rolfe, "and the
answer is yes."

"Oh, goody," said Rebecca giving her mother a hug.
"Well, I guess I better go down to the barn and make
friends with the animals. Goodbye, Mom."

"Goodbye, darling," said Mrs. Rolfe with tears in
her eyes.

Mrs. Piggle-Wiggle said, "Now don't worry, Mrs.
Rolfe. Rebecca and I are old friends and we'll get
along beautifully."

"I know you will," said Mrs. Rolfe sniffing. "But
I'm lonely for Rebecca already."

She got in her car and drove away. Rebecca waved
at her from the hayloft door.

All animals know when somebody loves them and is
not afraid of them and Mrs. Piggle-Wiggle's animals
adored Rebecca immediately. She could even get right
in the pen with Fanny and her piggies which was very
remarkable because Fanny was quite disagreeable and
usually tried to bite anyone who came in her pen. Lester, Wag and Lightfoot of course loved her and followed her all over the farm. Even Warren the gander
wasn't too nasty to her and only hissed when he was a
long way off. She curried Trotsky until he shone like
satin and then she led him out to the watering trough

and scrubbed his hoofs with soap and a stiff scrubbing brush. She gave Lester a bath with shampoo, rubbed him dry with one of Mrs. Piggle-Wiggle's bath towels and put lily of the valley cologne behind his ears.

She cleaned out all the stalls in the barn and put in fresh new straw. She cleaned out the chicken houses and put in fresh peat moss. She made a little pen for Fanny's babies out in the orchard, turned Fanny into Lester's pen, scrubbed Fanny's pen out with hot soap and water and covered the floor with clean sweet-smelling sawdust. She tidied up Penelope's cage and cleaned out the rabbit hutches and the turkey pens. She was busy and helpful and happy.

"I just don't know how I ran this farm without you," Mrs. Piggle-Wiggle told her. "Especially now that you have learned to milk."

"I'd like to live here forever," Rebecca said. "I love farms and I love animals and I love you."

Wag licked her hand, Lightfoot jumped onto her shoulder and Penelope said, "We love Rebecca. We love beautiful Rebecca."

Everything was just as happy as could be for one week. Then came the day when Mrs. Piggle-Wiggle had to take Lester in to the Hendricks' to cure Eunice of her bad table manners.

Mrs. Piggle-Wiggle had to leave very early because the 6:30 bus was the only one that came through Little Spring Valley. She told Rebecca that she would try to be home before dark.

Rebecca said, "Don't worry, Mrs. Piggle-Wiggle.

I'll feed the animals and milk Arbutus. Shall I turn Trotsky into the south pasture with the sheep?"

"That would be fine," said Mrs. Piggle-Wiggle. "And don't forget Heather's calf meal and be sure the baby chicks and ducklings and goslings are in before dark. You know how anxious Pulitzer, the owl, is to get his claws on them. Oh, yes, there is a pail of sour milk in the cellar to mix with Fanny's food. Well, I guess I'd better be off or I'll miss my bus. Come, Lester."

Rebecca hugged and kissed Mrs. Piggle-Wiggle and Lester and waved at them until her arm ached. Then she started down to the barn.

She was just going to turn on the water in the watering trough when she heard a funny noise down by the oat field. It was kind of a chug chug chug like a steam engine. She strained her eyes but she couldn't quite see because the chicken house was in the way. So she ran to the top of the hill and a big maple tree was in the way. Finally she ran all the way down to the oat field. Still she couldn't see anything. So she ran through the oat field until she came to the line fence and there just beyond in Mr. Larsen's wheat field was a big red tractor standing still and puffing.

"Hi, there," called Rebecca to the tractor.

"Hi," answered a voice from the back wheel. "I've lost a pin somewhere, do you want to help me look for it?"

"Sure," said Rebecca. "What kind of a pin, safety or straight?"

A big tall man stood up and laughed. He said, "It's a cotter pin. Sort of a nail with two prongs on it."

"Oh, I know," said Rebecca. "There's one on my bike. I fix my bike all the time."

"Good for you," said the man. "My name is Nels Larsen. What's yours?"

"Rebecca Rolfe," said Rebecca. "I'm visiting Mrs. Piggle-Wiggle."

"That's fine," said Nels. "She's a very nice woman. I'm going to cut her oats for her when they are ripe."

"Can I help you?" asked Rebecca.

"You sure can," said Nels. "Now let's look for that pin so I can finish my disking."

After almost half an hour of looking Rebecca found the pin and as a reward Nels let her ride on the tractor with him. At lunch time he took her home to his house and Mrs. Larsen gave her hot fresh bread, chicken and dumplings and wild blackberry pie. She had a wonderful time. But she had forgotten all about Mrs. Piggle-Wiggle's animals.

Arbutus was bawling in her stall waiting to be milked and fed. Trotsky stood in his stall whinnying to be fed and let out to pasture. Fanny and her piggies all squealed and grunted for their breakfast. The chickens cackled and cackled and Egbert shrieked "Breakfast" at the top of his voice. Warren and Evelyn Goose and Millard and Martha Mallard brought their babies over to the watering trough for a swim but there was no water. Rebecca had forgotten to turn it on.

Lightfoot meowed and meowed in the barn door but her saucer stayed dry. Wag barked and barked and barked but nobody filled his water dish. Georgette, Layette and Paulette brought their babies up by the back porch to see why Mrs. Piggle-Wiggle hadn't thrown them any grain and why they didn't have any water. Heather bawled and bawled for her breakfast, and Clematis and her lambs came clear up from the south pasture to see what was the matter.

Over at the Larsens' Rebecca shouted, "Giddayup, Charlie," as she guided the old white horse between the rows of potatoes. She was covered with dirt and perspiration and her face was as red as a tomato, but she was having a wonderful time. It was almost six o'clock when Nels finally told her that she'd better bring Charlie in for his supper.

"Supper! Oh, my gosh!" said Rebecca. "Oh, my gosh, I forgot to feed the animals and I forgot to milk Arbutus and I forgot to turn Trotsky into the pasture. Oh, what will I do?"

"You'd better run home as fast as your legs can carry you," said Nels. "It sounds to me as if you are in trouble. Listen."

Through the still evening air, across the rolling green fields, from Mrs. Piggle-Wiggle's farm came all kinds of loud cries for food.

"FOOOOOOOOOOOOOOOD!" bellowed Arbutus.

"MAAAAAAAAAAAAAAAALK," cried Heather.

"OH, oh, oh, oh, oh, oats," whinnied Trotsky.

"Ga, ga, ga, ga, graaaaaaaaaain," cackled the hens.

"Waaaaaaaaaaaaaaaaaaaaaaaaaaater," bleated the sheep.

"Meowlk, meeeeeeeeowlk!" whined Lightfoot.

"Food, food, food," barked Wag.

"Feed me, feed me, feed, me!" shrieked Penelope.

"She-forgot-our FOOD! She-forgot-our FOOD!" crowed Egbert.

"Lunch, lunch, lunch, lunch," grunted Fanny.

"Feeeeeeeed meeeeee! Feeeeeeeed meeeeee! Feeeeeeeed meeeeee! Feeeeeeeed meeeeee! Feeeeeeeed meeeeee! Feeeeeeeed meeeeee! Feeeeeeeed meeeeee! Feeeeeeeed meeeeee! Feeeeeeeed meeeeee! Feeeeeeeed meeeeee! Feeeeeeeed meeeeee! Feeeeeeeed meeeeee! Feeeeeeeed meeeeee!" squealed the fourteen piglets.

"Wheeeeee! Wheeeee! Wheeeeeeeeet!" whistled the turkey poults.

"We want to gobble-gobble-gobble-gobble! We want to gobble-gobble-gobble!" said Tom.

"Shame sssssssssssss! Shame sssssssssssss!" said Warren Gander.

"Come baaaaaaaack! Come baaaaaaaaaaaaaaak!" called Martha and Millard Mallard.

Rebecca hung her head. "I'm so ashamed," she said. "I forgot my friends."

"Well being ashamed won't help," Nels said. "Just hurry along home and feed them."

"Goodbye, Nels," Rebecca said. "It was awfully nice of you to let me ride the tractor and steer your horse."

"It was a pleasure," Nels said. "Come over any time."

Like a swallow Rebecca darted through the potato patch, across the wheat field, squeezed under the barbed-wire fence tearing the right leg of her jeans,

across the oat field, over the little hill, past the chicken house and into the barn. The noise in there was deafening. Wag saw her first. He dashed down from the house, raced through the door, and ran between her legs knocking her flat. Then instead of licking her face in apology he stood and growled at her.

She said, "Oh, Wag, please, forgive me, I'm truly sorry. I didn't mean to forget your food."

Coldly he turned away and went into Trotsky's stall.

Rebecca got up, hurried into the feed room, scooped up a lard bucket of mash and dumped it into Arbutus' feed box. She said, "I'm truly sorry, Arbutus. I'll milk you right away." Arbutus turned her head away.

45

Then Rebecca skittered up the loft stairs and threw down oat hay until Trotsky's manger was full. Peering down the chute at him, she said, "Oh, Trotsky, please forgive me." Trotsky turned his back on her.

Next she raced up to the house and got the slops and bucket of sour milk for Fanny. There were two full buckets and she had quite a time carrying them. She was panting when she got to Fanny's pen. "Here Fanny, old girl," she said, dumping in the whole bucket of clabbered milk.

"Grrrrrrr," said Fanny snapping at her hand.

"Why, Fanny, how could you?" Rebecca said begining to cry.

"Blup, blup, blup," said Fanny burying her snout in the milk. Rebecca poured in the other bucket, wiped her eyes on her sleeve and went in to milk Arbutus.

Arbutus' bag was swollen and she was leaking milk all over the floor. Rebecca felt very ashamed. She was milking as fast as she could and the milk was swishing into the bucket when she felt a sharp pain in her leg. She looked down and Lightfoot, tail switching, eyes blazing, was standing with one paw up ready to scratch her again. Quickly Rebecca got up, and filled Lightfoot's saucer with warm milk. She filled it three times before she finished milking.

Heather was so hungry she slurped up half the warm milk before Rebecca could mix the calf meal with it. As soon as she had fed Heather, Rebecca strained the rest of the milk, put it to cool, gave Arbutus some hay, brought her two buckets of water, cleaned out her stall and put in fresh straw. Then she went in to Trotsky.

As soon as she stepped into his stall he backed up and stepped on her foot. "Ow," she cried. "Trotsky, you are hurting me."

Looking around at her disdainfully he slowly lifted his hoof. Limping Rebecca brought him two buckets of water which he gulped down. Then she cleaned out his stall, put in fresh straw and gave him a bucket of oats. She didn't dare go in Fanny's pen but as the piggies were still nursing she knew they had plenty of food.

Then she hurried down to the chicken house. All the chickens had gone to bed but she filled the mash hoppers and scattered grain around for the early risers. There were two hens on the nests and when she reached under them to gather the eggs they pecked her wrists hard. After she had taken care of the chickens Rebecca fed the ducks and geese, the rabbits and the mother hens. Then she watered the sheep. Heavens, but she was tired and hungry! She went up to the house. Immediately Penelope shrieked at her, "Well, about time, Miss Gadding all day. Where's supper? Where's supper? Where's supper?"

"Please, dear, dear, dear Penelope, forgive me," Rebecca said. "I'll get your supper right away." She tried to open the back door but it was locked. "What will I do, poor Penelope?" she said rattling the doorknob. Then, on the bench by the pump, she saw the box of Parrot Crunch. "Now you poor dear little hungry parrot," she said dumping a cupful into Penelope's feeding cup.

Penelope hopped down off her perch, reached

47

through the bars of her cage and bit Rebecca's finger. "Ouch," Rebecca yelled.

"Serves you right, bad girl," Penelope said.

Wag came up on the back porch and barked at her. "Quiet, dog," Penelope yelled. "I'm eating."

"Yap, yap, yap," Wag said, sitting down on Rebecca's feet.

"Oh, poor Waggy," she said. "You want your supper. I'll go in the house and get it if you'll get off my feet." Wag obligingly moved. Rebecca tried to open the back door but it was still locked.

"I'll get you a drink of water, anyway," she said going over to the pump. She was priming the pump when to her surprise she saw Wag's dish filled with dog food in the sink. "Gosh, Mrs. Piggle-Wiggle never forgets anything," she said lifting out the dish and setting it on the floor. Wag rushed over and began to choke down the food.

Rebecca pumped him a bowl of water, filled Penelope's water dish and then went around to the front of the house to see if that door was locked too. It was. "That's funny," Rebecca said. "Mrs. Piggle-Wiggle doesn't usually lock her doors." She tried the windows, they were locked too. So feeling very hungry and very neglected, she went around and sat down on the back steps to wait for Mrs. Piggle-Wiggle.

Like giant black cobwebs dusk settled over the willow tree, the barn, the chicken house, the tool shed, the orchard trees. A big yellow moon came up from behind the Larsens' peach orchard. In the swampy place down the lane a million little frogs began to trill. The

animals were all quiet now. Except for the frogs everything was quiet. Quiet and lonely. Two large tears rolled out of Rebecca's nice brown eyes and slid down over her rosy cheeks. Wag came over and lay down beside her. Burrying her head in his fur she said, "I'm hungry and lonely and I think Mrs. Piggle-Wiggle has forgotten all about me." Turning his head around Wag licked her cheek, which only made Rebecca feel more sorry for herself and cry louder.

Then suddenly the quietness of the night was shattered into a million pieces. The ducks began to quack. The geese honked. Layette, Paulette and Georgette shrieked hysterically. Wag barked. Trotsky neighed. Lightfoot meowed.

"What is it? What's the matter?" Rebecca said to Wag.

"It's Pulitzer, the owl," Penelope said yawning. "He's after the baby chickens or the goslings or the ducklings. There he goes past the moon. He can't do any harm, though. All the babies are shut up."

"Oh, no they aren't!" said Rebecca jumping off the porch. "Oh here he comes. Shoo, shoo, Pulitzer. Go away, you bad owl!" she shouted, grabbing the broom and running down to the willow tree where all the commotion seemed to be.

Down Pulitzer swooped as quiet and dark as a shadow. He was heading right for the goslings. His wicked claws were opened ready to snatch up one of the small downy bodies.

Running so fast she was almost flying, Rebecca didn't see Warren who with wings outstretched was bravely trying to guard his babies. Rebecca fell right over him and landed with a splash in the watering trough. But as she fell she managed to clout Pulitzer hard with the broom. He zigzagged for a minute or two then swooped up to the ridgepole of the barn. After she had scrambled out of the watering trough, Rebecca picked up her broom, herded all the chickens, geese and ducks into the barn and shut the door. Then shaking her fist up at Pulitzer she said, "You keep away from here, you mean old thing."

Pulitzer said, "Hoo, hoo, hoo!" and flew into the orchard.

Just then Mrs. Piggle-Wiggle's flashlight came bobbing along the lane like a lightning bug. Rebecca, Wag

and Lightfoot ran to meet her. After she had kissed and petted them all she said, "My goodness, Rebecca, you feel a little wet. What happened?" So Rebecca told her everything. How she had forgotten to feed and water the animals, how she had forgotten to milk, how she had forgotten to shut up the goslings, ducklings and chicks and Pulitzer had almost gotten them.

Mrs. Piggle-Wiggle said, "Well, everything has been taken care of and old Pulitzer didn't get anything so what do you say we wipe away the tears and go in the house?"

"But we can't," Rebecca said. "We can't get in the

house. The doors are all locked and I can't find the key."

"Oh, how careless of me," said Mrs. Piggle-Wiggle. "I forgot and locked the doors. That means you haven't had any supper. You poor child."

Rebecca began to cry again. "I'm freezing and starving," she sobbed.

"It's amazing how uncomfortable it is to be forgotten," said Mrs. Piggle-Wiggle fishing in her purse for her door key. "Now you run up and put on your nightie and I'll make hot cocoa and toast. I think there's some cold fried chicken in the pantry and I know there's some gingerbread."

Of course that was the last time Rebecca ever forgot about a pet. When she went home at the end of two weeks, Mrs. Piggle-Wiggle trusted her so much she gave her Brookfield, the little runt pig, a gosling named Gordon, a duckling called Dalrymple and two baby chickens, Chauncy and Chervil.

When her daddy saw Rebecca he was very happy, but when he saw her new pets he made a kind of mournful groan, slammed the door to his study and said, "No more rest for me, I can see that."

But he was wrong. From that day on Rebecca took perfect care of her pets and they were so well behaved that Mrs. Piggle-Wiggle often sent other Pet Forgetters to visit Rebecca so they could see how pets should be cared for.

## III. THE DESTRUCTIVENESS CURE

"WHO'S BEEN MONKEYING WITH THE LAWN MOWER?" shouted Mr. Phillips from the garage.

"Did you call, Hearthrug dear?" said Mrs. Phillips from the vegetable garden where she was weeding her radishes.

"YES, I CALLED," said Mr. Phillips. "WHO HAS BEEN FOOLING WITH THE LAWN MOWER? ONE WHEEL IS MISSING, THE BOLTS ARE GONE FROM THE HANDLE AND THERE ARE BALL BEARINGS ALL OVER THE GARAGE FLOOR!"

"Oh, dear," said Mrs. Phillips, getting up off her knees and sighing deeply. "I suppose it was Jeffie. He was playing in there yesterday."

"TELL HIM TO COME HERE," roared Mr. Phillips.

"I can't," said Mrs. Phillips. "He's gone to spend the day with Billy Robinson."

"CALL UP THE ROBINSONS!" growled Mr. Phillips. "Call up the Robinsons and tell them to send our destroying angel home."

"I can't," said Mrs. Phillips coming into the garage. She bent over and started to gather the ball bearings up in her gardening basket.

"Leave those alone, Sybil," said Mr. Phillips. "Leave those for Jeff. I've had just about enough of his destroying things. From now on and starting with this lawn mower he is putting things back together."

"But Hearthrug, dear, do you think he can?" asked Mrs. Phillips looking at the garage floor which was littered with about 400 tiny lawn mower parts.

"I don't care whether he can or not, he's GOING TO!" said Mr. Phillips, his eyes blazing. "Go call the Robinsons!"

"It won't do any good," said Mrs. Phillips, "because Orrisroot Robinson has driven the children to Green River Falls for the day. They have taken a picnic and won't be home until eight o'clock tonight."

"Well," said Mr. Phillips, "that's a fine state of affairs. Gone on a picnic! A reward, I suppose, for tearing the lawn mower to pieces. That's the trouble with children today. When they misbehave they are not punished, they are rewarded."

"Now, Hearthrug," said Mrs. Phillips. "Please be reasonable. I didn't send Jeff to the Robinsons as a reward for taking the lawn mower apart. I didn't know he had. I sent him to the Robinsons because Orrisroot called and invited him. Today is Billy's tenth birthday and the picnic is his party. Now as long as you can't cut the lawn why don't you just go and lie down in the lawn swing? I'll make you a pitcher of lemonade."

"All right," said Mr. Phillips. "I was really too tired to cut the lawn anyway. Say, as long as you are in the kitchen, how about making me a root beer ice-cream soda?"

"Of course, dear," said Mrs. Phillips. "And would you like a bologna sandwich to go with it?"

"I guess so," said Mr. Phillips walking over and sinking weakly down into the lawn swing. "But be sure and put plenty of mustard on the bread, use that Russian rye I brought home yesterday, and don't forget the dill pickles."

"All right, dear," said Mrs. Phillips.

"And, Sybil," called Mr. Phillips as Mrs. Phillips went into the kitchen, "better make it two sandwiches and don't forget the lettuce and mayonnaise."

"Yes, dear," said Mrs. Phillips.

After Mrs. Phillips had made the sandwiches, using plenty of mustard and not forgetting the lettuce and mayonnaise, or the pickles, she got out the ice cream and the root beer for the root beer ice-cream soda. Then she opened the cupboard where she kept her electric blender. The cupboard was empty. The blender was not there.

"Could I have loaned the blender to someone?" Mrs. Phillips wondered opening cupboard after cupboard. Going out on the back porch she called to Mr. Phillips in the lawn swing, "Hearthrug, darling, do you remember my loaning my electric blender to anyone?"

"If you did it was either this morning or after twelve o'clock last night," said Mr. Phillips, "because I made myself a chocolate malt at eleven-thirty last night."

"Oh, of course, I remember," said Mrs. Phillips. "And you didn't wash it and left the drainboard half an inch deep in chocolate syrup, malted milk and melted ice cream."

Mr. Phillips closed his eyes wearily.

Going back in the house Mrs. Phillips again began her search for the blender.

Finally after half an hour, when she realized it just wasn't to be found, she ran across the street to borrow Mrs. Harpoon's blender. Mrs. Harpoon said, "Certainly you can borrow my blender, Sybil, but I thought Jeffie said he had yours fixed. He was working on it early this morning."

"Where was he working on it?" asked Mrs. Phillips.

"Out in our garage," said Mrs. Harpoon. "My goodness he and Donnie were out there at a little after six."

With a sinking heart Mrs. Phillips walked out to the Harpoons' garage. There on the work bench in about fifty pieces was her nice new blender.

She said, "Do you have a paper bag I can borrow, Heather?"

"Certainly," said Mrs. Harpoon. "My but that little Jeffie of yours is a wonderful mechanic. Really, I think he is a genius. He is so thorough."

"He is thorough, anyway," said Mrs. Phillips, gathering up all the tiny little parts of the blender and putting them in the paper bag.

"Well, thanks, Heather," she said. "I'll bring your blender home the minute I'm finished with it and please, whatever you do, *never ever, let Jeffie touch it.*"

Mr. Phillips was pretty cross at having to wait so long for his lunch so Mrs. Phillips didn't say anything to him about the blender, instead she put the paper bag in the cupboard and wrote a note on her shopping list, "Take blndr. pts. bk. to stre. to see if can be fixt."

After he had had his lunch and a restful nap, Mr. Phillips felt much better and decided to try and put the lawn mower back together himself. Humming, he went down to the basement to get his tools. A minute later he came roaring into the kitchen, his face purple, in his hands the pieces of his brace and bit, and the pieces of his level. "LOOK!" he shouted. "JUST LOOK! MY BEST TOOLS AND THEY ARE RUINED!"

Mrs. Phillips said, "Don't complain to me, Hearthrug, I just went to get out the vacuum cleaner and it is in ten thousand pieces, the carpet sweeper is in sixty pieces and here," she jerked open the cupboard where she had put the parts of the blender, "here is my brand new electric blender." She began to cry.

Putting his broken tools on the drainboard of the sink, Mr. Phillips peered into the paper bag of blender parts, then said, "Sybil, I'm going to buy a razor strap. The biggest, strongest one made and I'm going to beat the destructiveness out of that boy."

Mrs. Phillips cried even louder. She said, "Beating is barbaric, and I won't have it."

"All right then," said Mr. Phillips. "What would you suggest?"

"I don't know," sobbed Mrs. Phillips. "I don't know but there must be something better than a razor strap."

"There is nothing wrong with a razor strap," said Mr. Phillips.

"That isn't the answer at all," said Mrs. Phillips. "I'm going to ask Greta Rockstall what to do. She has eight children."

"Do whatever you please," said Mr. Phillips, "but

don't come crying to me when you find your sewing machine or your electric iron, or your waffle iron or your toaster or your . . ."

"Hearthrug, please," said Mrs. Phillips, dialing the telephone number of her friend Greta Rockstall.

When she told Greta all the terrible things Jeffie had done Greta laughed and said, "We had the very same trouble with Wickie. He took our phonograph and our electric mixer apart and then got the parts mixed up and when they were put back together the mixer played music and the phonograph ground up the records. And another time he put the power lawn mower motor on the baby carriage, and started it, that was when Electra was only four months old, and she went clear to Centerville and we didn't know a thing about it until a garage man called and said the baby carriage was out of gas and what did we want to do about it. He got our name from Electra's identification tag."

"Oh, my goodness, that's the most terrible thing I ever heard of," said Mrs. Phillips. "What did you do, I mean how did you punish him?"

"I sent him to Mrs. Piggle-Wiggle," said Mrs. Rockstall. "She is so wonderful with children and always seems to know just how to cure their faults."

"Of course," said Mrs. Phillips with such a big sigh of relief it blew the leaves of the telephone book over to Ney-Niebruegge. "I can't imagine why I didn't think of Mrs. Piggle-Wiggle myself. Goodness knows Jeffie used to spend enough time at her house. Is she still living at the same place?"

"No she isn't," said Mrs. Rockstall. "She has a farm now. It is in Little Spring Valley just at the edge of town. Her number is in the phone book, though. Why don't you call her right now, Sybil? It will be such a relief to your mind."

"I will," said Mrs. Phillips. "Thank you so much for your help, Greta. I'll let you know what Mrs. Piggle-Wiggle says."

Tuesday morning as soon as she finished milking, Mrs. Piggle-Wiggle hurried up to the house and began making buckwheat cakes and cooking little pig sausages. The sausages were just beginning to brown when Mrs. Phillips' station wagon turned into the lane. Mrs.

Piggle-Wiggle, Wag, and Lightfoot went out on the back porch to wait for Jeffie. The car had barely stopped when he jumped out, ran up the back steps and gave Mrs. Piggle-Wiggle a big hug.

"I'm certainly glad you came early," Mrs. Piggle-Wiggle said. "I'm baking buckwheat cakes and I've got fresh honey."

"Oh, boy," Jeffie said. "Well, goodbye, Mom."

"Goodbye nothing," said Mrs. Piggle-Wiggle. "I've invited your mother for breakfast."

"But I mustn't stay," said Mrs. Phillips. "I have a meeting of the Driftwood Polishers, Bleachers and Arrangers at noon, and I promised Stella Packinghouse I would bring a casserole dish. I think I'll make my famous prune, noodle, sardine surprise."

"Ugh," said Jeffie. "How many sausages can I have, Mrs. Piggle-Wiggle?"

"It is 'May I,'" said Mrs. Phillips. "And don't be such a pig."

"Would eleven be enough?" asked Mrs. Piggle-Wiggle. "If it isn't I'll cook more."

"Zowie!" said Jeffie.

"Well, goodbye," said Mrs. Phillips. "Please be good and do as Mrs. Piggle-Wiggle tells you and try not to eat her out of house and home."

"What do you mean by that?" asked Jeffie, stuffing three sausages in his mouth.

"I mean," said his mother, "that you should eat your sausages one at a time and you should cut them in pieces instead of stuffing them into your mouth whole."

"Okay," said Jeffie waving at her.

But after his mother had driven away he ate fourteen buckwheat cakes and fourteen sausages and while he ate he told Mrs. Piggle-Wiggle all the news about all the children in the town. He knew all the Brownie Scouts who had flown up and were Girl Scouts and all the Cub Scouts who had climbed up and were Boy Scouts. He knew who was mad at whom and why and who was best friends with whom and why. He even knew the exact day that Patsy's grandmother was coming from New Orleans, and that Susan Gray was going to have the braces taken off her teeth on the seventh of August. Mrs. Piggle-Wiggle enjoyed her breakfast so much she almost forgot to put Arbutus out in the pasture. "Heavens to Betsy," she said jumping up. "Here it is seven-thirty and I haven't finished my chores."

"What chores?" said Jeffie. "Can I help. I'll drive that old cow."

So he and Mrs. Piggle-Wiggle went down to the barn and while Mrs. Piggle-Wiggle cleaned up the milk room, he turned Arbutus into the south pasture, petted Clematis and the lambs, fed Fanny and watched the piggies. He enjoyed himself very much.

Then Mrs. Piggle-Wiggle had to go up to the house and order some more calf meal and so she told Jeffie to amuse himself until she came back. He amused himself by undoing all the straps on Trotsky's bridle, taking the stirrups off the saddle, taking the pins out of the wheels on Mrs. Piggle-Wiggle's old farm cart, and with the blade of his pocketknife, loosening the screws that fastened the hinges on the door to Fanny's pen. When Mrs. Piggle-Wiggle came back she handed Jeffie a small toolbox. She said, "This is my toolbox. I understand you are very good at fixing things so while you are visiting me I'll just put you in charge of the tools and when anything gets broken you can fix it."

"Oh, boy," Jeffie said. "I like to fix things."

"That's splendid," Mrs. Piggle-Wiggle said. "While I gather the eggs and feed the chickens you take a look around and see if anything needs fixing."

So Jeffie took the toolbox and went importantly up to the watering trough and in no time at all he had broken off the faucet handle so that it was impossible to turn the water either off or on. Then he went up on the back porch, took the pump all apart, undid the doorbell so that it wouldn't ring, dismantled a small churn, loosened the screw eyes that held up the porch swing, and finally took apart the toolbox itself which was metal and put together with very nice hinges. He was sitting in the sunshine taking apart his Micky Mouse wrist watch when Mrs. Piggle-Wiggle came up from the barn. She said, "Did you find anything that needed fixing, Jeffie?"

"Yeah," he said. "The faucet of the watering trough worked kind of hard. I tried to fix it, but I kind of broke off the handle."

"That's too bad," she said, "because we can't get a new handle until we go to town Thursday. However, until we get a new handle you can pump water here on the porch, and carry it down to the trough. The buckets are there on the bench."

"Well, you see, I mean, uh, that is, uh," said Jeffie. "I figured the pump wasn't working just right and so

I took it apart and I'm not sure I can put it back together."

"Oh, mercy," said Mrs. Piggle-Wiggle, walking over and looking at the pump which was strewn all over the bench. "Well, in that case I guess you'll just have to carry water from the spring. It is up behind the house. You go out past the woodshed and follow that little trail until you get to it. Here, you had better take two buckets."

She handed Jeffie two twelve-quart milk buckets.

Whistling rather tunelessly he jumped off the porch and ran across the back yard.

"Hey, this is fun," he said to himself. "I bet that ole spring's got bullfrogs in it and maybe a big swimming hole."

He started up the path. It was very narrow and overgrown with blackberries and nettles.

"Hey, ouch," Jeffie yelled as a blackberry vine grabbed him around the arm and made a long red scratch on his flesh. He hit at the vine with the bucket and a nettle bent down and stung him on the back of the neck. "Hey, this is awful," he said as a mosquito bit him on the nose. "Why doesn't somebody cut this ole path?"

"Because we seldom have to use it," said Mrs. Piggle-Wiggle from behind him. "Here let me by and I'll sickle you a path. I had better make it nice and broad because you will be using it a great deal. Animals drink an enormous amount of water, you know."

The spring was pretty. It bubbled coolly and Jeffie did see a big bullfrog but the path down to the spring

was slippery and there were lots of mosquitoes and with a bucket of water in each hand he couldn't slap at them. Once he tried but the water slopped over and filled his shoe. He found that water is the heaviest, sloppiest, hardest thing in the world to carry and what was worse, Trotsky alone could drink a bucket with one slurp.

All the long hot afternoon Jeffie staggered back and forth from the spring. He was hot and itchy and stung all over with nettles. Then he had an idea. Ho, ho, he had it. He would hitch Trotsky to the cart and drive back and forth from the spring. Gosh, with Trotsky he could carry four ten gallon milk cans of water at a time. This would be easy.

The first blow of course was the harness which he had taken apart so thoroughly that morning. For an

64

hour he buckled and unbuckled but he couldn't seem to get it just right. So then he thought, "I'll just pull the cart myself. I won't be able to carry milk cans of water but I can carry about four buckets at a time."

So he lugged the cart across the barnyard, past the house and up to the spring. It was very very hard work and when he finally got it up to the spring he was so hot he had to lie down and slap cold water on his forehead. After he had cooled off he filled the four buckets, loaded them in the cart and started home. Pulling the cart with the four buckets of water in it was quite a job, even for a husky nine-year-old boy.

"It's this darn path," Jeffie kept saying to himself, as he pushed and pulled and jounced along. "As soon as I get to Mrs. Piggle-Wiggle's yard it will be easy as pie."

When he finally got to Mrs. Piggle-Wiggle's yard the left wheel came off the cart, the cart tipped over and all the water spilled. Jeffie was so mad he kicked the wagon wheel as hard as he could which was a mistake because he had on tennis shoes. "Ouch," he shrieked. "Ouch, my toe is broken. Help, help, I'm in agony."

"What in the world is the matter?" asked Mrs. Piggle-Wiggle from the porch where she was shelling peanuts for peanut brittle.

"My toe," Jeffie yelled. "I've broken it."

"Well come here on the porch and let me take a look at it," said Mrs. Piggle-Wiggle.

The toe was very red and swollen but Mrs. Piggle-Wiggle wiggled it and said she didn't think it was broken. She made Jeffie lie in the hammock and gave him six large fresh ginger-cookies and a glass of lemonade for medicine. He said he felt much better right away. As soon as she finished the peanuts Mrs. Piggle-Wiggle called up Mr. Larsen and asked him if he had a spare faucet or perhaps could fix her pump. He said he would be right over.

Mrs. Piggle-Wiggle met him at the barn and talked to him for quite a while in a low voice. Then he came up, lifted Jeffie out of the hammock and carried him down to the watering trough, set him down on his good foot and said, "Now son, I'll tell you what to do, but you're going to fix this faucet. After all you were strong enough to take it apart so you should be smart enough to put it back together. Now first you take this Stillson wrench . . ."

When Jeffie had fixed the faucet and had filled the watering trough, Mr. Larsen carried him up to the porch and sat him on the bench by the pump. "Now, son," he said, "you're going to learn how to fix a pump."

By the time he had taught Jeffie how to fix the pump Mr. Larsen had to go home and milk.

He said, "It's all right though, I don't think you'll need me for anything else, Mrs. Piggle-Wiggle, this young feller is pretty handy with tools."

"Thanks, Mr. Larsen," Jeffie said, scratching a big mosquito bite on his leg. "Thanks ever so much for showing me how to fix the faucet and the pump."

"That's all right, Jeffie," said Mr. Larsen. "Some day you can come over and help me with my tractor."

"As soon as my toe gets well," Jeffie said. "I'll ride Trotsky over."

Then he remembered the bridle and his face turned brick red. He said, "Say Mrs. Piggle-Wiggle, are there any kind of instructions about putting bridles together? I mean buckling the right pieces to the right pieces."

Mrs. Piggle-Wiggle laughed. She said, "I guess there are, Jeffie, but I don't happen to have any. However, after supper I'll bring the bridle up here and show you how to put it back together."

While Mrs. Piggle-Wiggle was milking, Jeffie limped over to the steps, sat down and put the toolbox back together. Then he put all the tools neatly away. He felt better somehow. Then he remembered the churn and he fixed that. He was working on the doorbell when Mrs. Piggle-Wiggle called him to supper. After supper she showed him how to fix the bridle and then she made him soak his toe and go to bed.

He was very, very tired and his bed, with its cool white sheets and blue and white patchwork quilt looked so inviting he forgot about his toe and made a great big leap from the rug right into the middle. There was a terrible crash and he was lying squashed down between the springs and the mattress.

"What happened? Are you hurt?" asked Mrs. Piggle-Wiggle as she helped him out.

"I'm all right," Jeffie said sheepishly. "It's just that I guess I, uh, sort of forgot that I sort of loosened the screws in the bed this morning. I mean I was testing

out the screwdriver on my pocket knife to see if it was any good."

"Well, was it?" Mrs. Piggle-Wiggle asked, laughing.

"I guess so," said Jeffie.

"All right," said Mrs. Piggle-Wiggle. "Sore toe or not you'll have to help me lift this mattress and springs and put the bed back together. Where are the tools?"

"Right here," said Jeffie limping over and getting the toolbox off the window seat.

So they put the bed back together and Mrs. Piggle-Wiggle made it all fresh and finally tucked Jeffie in. All night long he dreamed of boiling hot deserts without water and blackberry vines with thorns as big as daggers. He spent most of the next day lying in the hammock and soaking his toe.

But the day after that he was much better and before breakfast had fixed the wheels of the cart and tightened up all the bolts on the mowing machine. After breakfast while Mrs. Piggle-Wiggle did her chores, he mended a broken place in the fence, nailed down a loose step, fixed a wiggly leg on a kitchen chair and repaired the latch on the screen door. Mrs. Piggle-Wiggle told him she was very proud of him. After lunch Mrs. Piggle-Wiggle walked over to Mrs. Larsen's to get a bread-and-butter pickle recipe. She asked Jeffie to go along but he said that his toe still hurt a little and he didn't feel like walking. She told him to lie in the hammock and look at books and she would be home soon.

For a little while after she had gone Jeffie lay in the hammock and looked at the Sears Roebuck catalogue. Then he and Wag took a little walk down to the end of the lane. Then he played ball with Wag for a while. He'd throw the ball down the lane and Wag would run and bring it back. Then he threw stones at crows and the crows ducked and 'said, "Caw, Caw, Caw, Smarty." Then he caught a few bees in a fruit jar. Then he wandered down to the barn. He could hear Fanny snoring clear out in the barnyard. He limped over to her pen and looked in at her. "Gee, you're disgusting, Fanny," he said. "You're fat and dirty and you snore."

Fanny opened one small eye and looked at him. "Grrrrrrrrumph," she said and began to snore again.

"You make me sick," said Jeffie. "Just lying there and snoring. Why don't you wake up."

"Grrrrrrrrumph," Fanny said. The thirteen little pigs all crowded down at the end of the pen where Jeffie was, hoping he would have something delicious to eat for them.

"Want to get away from your big fat ugly mother for a while," he asked them.

"Yeeees, yeeees," they squealed.

So he opened the door into Lester's pen and they hurried through and began sniffing around in the straw hoping for little extra grains of wheat or hidden crusts. Jeffie watched them for a while until he grew tired, then he went back to lean over Fanny's pen and watch her. She was still snoring. For some reason this irritated Jeffie. "That ole pig's snorin' makes me sick at my stummick," he told Wag. "Why doesn't she get up and move around?"

Wag was busy sniffing at the piggies between the boards of Lester's pen and did not answer.

"Well I've got an idea," Jeffie said limping out to the willow tree and breaking off a branch. He took the branch back to Fanny's pen and began tickling her with it. It was just right for tickling—long and supple with a small bunch of leaves at the very end. At first Fanny who was used to flies and bugs didn't apparently feel the tickling. She snored on, her fat legs and small hooves stretched straight out in front of her. Then Jeffie tickled her on the end of the snout. She snorted a little. He kept on tickling. She opened one small eye. He kept on tickling. She got up with a roar and lunged at

70

him. The whole pen quivered but Jeffie laughed and flipped the willow switch at her. She lunged again but this time she hit the door to the pen. The very door whose hinges Jeffie had loosened the first day he came. The hinges came off, the door crashed open and Fanny was free.

Jeffie almost fainted. "Run, Wag, run. Fanny's out!" he shouted streaking for the barn door. Pigs are funny animals. They are big and fat and awkward and pig-gish but they can run like lightning. Especially mean old mother pigs. So when Jeffie reached the willow tree Fanny's snout and her sharp teeth were only about two inches from his leg. Giving a jump that took him at least four feet off the ground, Jeffie snagged a branch, swung both legs up over his head and grabbed a higher branch with his knees. He wasn't very comfortable but he was safe. Below him Fanny scratched her sides against the willow trunk and snarled. Wag, safe on the back porch, barked and barked. Jeffie's hands began to ache a little. He tried hanging by one hand. That made his arms ache. He wanted to get up by his knees so he wouldn't be hanging upside down. He tried giving a little swing with his body and the branch under his knees creaked alarmingly. My, he was uncomfortable! His face was as red as a fire engine and his toe ached.

"Where is Mrs. Piggle-Wiggle?" he said. Then he began to shout, "Help! help! help! Mrs. Piggle-Wiggle, save me!"

From above him in the tree Penelope said, "Oh, for heaven's sake, boy, quiet down. You're disturbing everyone."

"But I'm upside down," wailed Jeffie. "Help, help, HELP!" he shouted again.

"What in the world's the matter with you? If you don't like being upside down, why don't you get out of the tree?" Penelope said.

"Because Fanny's down there and she's going to bite me," said Jeffie beginning to bawl.

"Well, how did she get out?" Penelope asked. "She ought to be in her pen."

"She was," said Jeffie. "But I loosened the hinges on her door the first day I came and then I forgot all about it and I was tickling her on the nose and she

72

charged and the door came off and she almost bit me."

"Well, you're a mischievous boy and I don't have much sympathy for you," said Penelope, "but I don't like Fanny either so I'll help you. Now when I chase Fanny into the barn you get down out of this tree and shut the door. I'll get out the hayloft window."

"How can you chase Fanny?" Jeffie asked.

"Just watch and see," said Penelope.

There was a great clatter of wings and then a thump as she flew out of the willow tree and landed on the ground. Then in an exact imitation of Mrs. Piggle-Wiggle's voice she said, "Now, Fanny, get along, go on, get back in your pen. Hurry now, Fanny. Supper, Fanny, I've got your nice supper. Hurry, Fanny."

Fanny waddled into the barn. Like a flash Jeffie was out of the tree and rolling the big barn door shut. As he latched the door he could hear Penelope, "Nice girl, Fanny. Supper's ready."

Then from the loft window Penelope said, "Now, you foolish boy, you had better go up to the house and get your toolbox and the bucket of slops. I'll keep Fanny quiet until you get her food in the trough. Then while she is eating you put the hinges back on that door. All right now, scat, boy."

Jeffie scatted. He was pretty nervous about going in the barn but Penelope reminded him that if anything went wrong and Fanny started after him again, he could go up in the loft. "Anybody with an ounce of brains would have thought of that in the first place," she said.

Jeffie thought so too, and was ashamed because he had been so dumb. So carrying the bucket of slops in one hand and the toolbox under his arm, he squeezed through the barn door and tiptoed over to Fanny's pen. He could hear Penelope talking, "Quiet, now, girl. Supper's coming. Supper's coming."

As soon as he dumped in the bucket of slops Fanny lunged forward and buried her head in it. "Now," Penelope said, "quick, the door. Stand it up and fix those hinges."

Jeffie's hands shook so the screwdriver kept jumping out of the slot in the screws but finally he had one hinge on tight. With an anxious look at Fanny's trough which was almost empty, he started on the other. He just finished when Fanny turned around and saw him. "Grrrrrrrumph," she said and started toward him. Grabbing his toolbox, Jeffie ran to the ladder that went up to the loft.

"Don't worry, boy, the pen's holding," Penelope called out. She flew down from the rafter where she had been perched while directing things and waddled out to Jeffie. "Come on, boy," she said. "While you've got your tools out I wish you'd fix the door of my cage. It won't stay open and it won't stay shut."

When Mrs. Piggle-Wiggle got home a little later, Jeffie had finished fixing Penelope's cage and was tightening up the porch swing. He told Mrs. Piggle-Wiggle all about Fanny and how Penelope had saved his life and she said, "You're a good girl, Penelope, I'm proud of you. Here are some sunflower seeds."

"Delicious," said Penelope eating one. "I'll fly down this afternoon and thank her."

"Oh, Jeffie," said Mrs. Piggle-Wiggle, "Nels is going to work on the tractor this evening. He said to tell you to bring your toolbox and come over after supper."

"Oh, boy," said Jeffie. "I've always wanted to fix a tractor."

And that was how Jeffie Phillips learned that tools are for fixing things not just for taking them apart.

Today if you go down his street you will see a big sign, "JEFFIE PHILLIPS AND WICKIE ROCK-STALL REPAIR SHOP —— WE FIX ANYTHING!"

They get lots of business, too. Yesterday they put Patsy's big doll's eyes in, mended the broken chain on Dick Thompson's bicycle, and fixed Mrs. Harpoon's vacuum cleaner. They even helped Mr. Phillips clean the sparkplugs on his car. When they aren't fixing things they are building. The first thing they built was a beautiful doghouse for Wag. They took it out to Mrs. Piggle-Wiggle's farm last Sunday. She was simply delighted and Wag was so happy he licked Jeffie's ear and untied Wickie's shoe. While they were playing around the farm Jeffie noticed that the watering trough was getting kind of rotten in some places. They built a new, bigger one. Mrs. Piggle-Wiggle was very pleased and Penelope said, "Glad I saved you from Fanny. You're a good boy!"

75

## IV. THE FRAIDY-CAT CURE

"OH, DON'T turn off my light, Mother, please, don't," Phoebe Jackstraw wailed. "You know I'm afraid of the dark!"

"Of course I'm going to turn off your light," said Mrs. Jackstraw. "You can't sleep restfully with a light shining in your eyes."

"I can," Phoebe said, "and I can't sleep at all when it's dark and I think the bureau is a gorilla and the curtain is a witch and the lamp is a goblin."

"Now Phoebe, that is pure nonsense," said her mother snapping off the light. "Look, the bureau is just a bureau, the curtain is only a curtain being blown by the summer breeze and the lamp, if it looks like anything at all, looks like a little lady wearing a hoop skirt."

Phoebe sighed and said, "Well, don't shut the door then."

"All right," said her mother. "I'll leave the hall door open but I don't want you sneaking down and sitting on the stairs and listening."

"I only do that because I'm afraid," said Phoebe.

"Oh, Phoebe," said her mother, "how can you be afraid when you have three brothers sleeping in the next room?"

"Boys," said Phoebe. "Boys are no help. All they do is tease. Last night Jeremy hid behind my door and jumped out at me and I was so scared I spilled all my lilac bathpowder. And old Chuckie hides under my bed and pinches my legs and Georgie climbs out on the roof and comes in my window and scares me."

"Nobody would tease you if you weren't such a fraidy-cat," said Mrs. Jackstraw. "Now kiss me good night and go right to sleep."

Phoebe kissed her mother but she didn't go right to sleep. She lay in bed as stiff as an icicle and looked around the dark room with round scared eyes. She had forgotten to shut the closet door and she thought she could see a thin bony hand with long curved nails reaching out and feeling around. Was she imagining it? Oh, no, there it was again. She pulled the covers over her head. It was very hot and stuffy under the covers but at least the witch would have to kill her through the blankets.

Then there was a noise, a raspy, scrapy noise over by the window. A robber was cutting the screen and was coming in the window. And her gold beads and her wrist watch were right in plain sight on the bureau. Suddenly from outside the window came the most terrible noise—a cross between a moan of agony, a death wail and a cry for help. With a shriek Phoebe threw off the covers, tore out of her room, ran downstairs and burst in on her mother and father who were playing bridge with the Murphys. "Save me, save me!" Phoebe yelled. "My room is full of robbers and there's one being killed right outside my window."

"You take her upstairs, Henderson," said Mrs. Jackstraw. "You're dummy."

So Mr. Jackstraw took Phoebe's cold little hand, led her upstairs and into the robber's den. Turning on the bedside light he said, "Now, chickabiddy, show Daddy all the robbers and witches and killers."

"First came this terrible bony hand with long claws," said Phoebe pointing to the closet.

Mr. Jackstraw strode over, opened the closet door wide, pushed the hangers from one side to the other and said, "Nothing there at all. Are you sure you didn't see the arm of your bathrobe? It's white and it's kind of caught on the shoebag here. See how it comes out the door?"

"Oh, I guess that was it," said Phoebe, laughing

weakly. "But what about the robber that cut my screen and that awful noise."

Going over and examining the screen, Mr. Jackstraw said, "The screen is just like new but there is a branch of the rosebush here by the window. I imagine that a breeze could make it scrape against the screen and make a grating noise. Now what was the other dreadful thing, chickabiddy?"

"The noise," Phoebe said. "Kind of a moan, a howl, a shriek, a scream, a growl and a death wail."

"That's quite a combination," said Mr. Jackstraw. "The owner should patent it. Now where did this unusual sound come from?"

"Right outside my window," said Phoebe. "Oh, it was terrible, Daddy. It made my blood all cold and lumpy."

"You mean," said Mr. Jackstraw, "all cold and lumpy like Sarah's oatmeal?"

"Now, Daddy," said Phoebe, "you're making fun of me."

"On the contrary," said her daddy, "I'm just attempting to establish the facts in the case. Remember I'm a lawyer."

"All right," said Phoebe. "Now that you have established the facts what was the noise?"

"I don't know," said her father peering out the window. "I can't see anything unusual out here except your bicycle which should be in the garage. Perhaps it is afraid of the dark too and was crying for you to let it in."

"Now Daddy," said Phoebe, "you're just being silly. Bicycles don't have voices unless they have horns. The bony hand was my imagination and I guess I imagined that there was a robber cutting the screen but I didn't imagine that terrible noise. It was a kind of moan, howl, scream, and wail. It was just awful."

"Well," said her father, "there is nothing visible from this window that could have produced such a noise but if it will make you happy, I will go down and prowl around outside. Why don't you watch me from the window. I'll put a white flower in my buttonhole so you will be able to tell me from the crowd of killers and robbers that are always hanging around this house."

So Phoebe, knelt by the window and shivered and watched while her daddy, wearing a white camellia in his buttonhole, looked behind every bush, and tree, walked up and down the street and even searched inside the Murphy's car. "All right, baby," he called up to her. "Hop into bed now. All the screamers, howlers and wailers seem to have gone home."

So Phoebe got into bed and turned off her light and was just about asleep when, "Woooo, wooo, awooooooo, eeeeeeee, ohooooooooooooh," came the terrible noise. Like a bullet she shot out of bed, took the steps two at a time, leapt into her daddy's arms.

"The noise, Daddy," she wailed. "The terrible noise. Listen!"

They listened and sure enough they could hear a strange noise that was sort of a cross between a wail, a moan, a howl, a growl and a scream.

Dumping Phoebe off his lap Mr. Jackstraw strode over and opened the front door. Then he began to laugh and called, "Come here everybody. Here is the culprit."

They all ran to the door and there sitting in a pool of moonlight was a red and white dog howling at the moon. "Oh, that is the Weskits' pointer," Mrs. Murphy said. "They have gone on a little trip and they asked me to feed and water him. I guess he was lonely and followed us here. Come Bobo. Come Bobo."

The hunting dog turned, gave Mrs. Murphy a sorrowful look, tilted back his head and let forth the most mournful, the most agonized, the most heart-rending wail anyone had ever heard. Then he walked solemnly over and lay down under the Murphys' car.

"So that's why I couldn't find you before," Mr. Jackstraw said. "All right old boy, lie under the car if you want to but please don't sing any more. Phoebe can't stand your voice."

"Wunh, wush, warhw," said Bobo, his head on his paws.

Giving Phoebe a hug, Mr. Jackstraw said, "Now that I've caught all your killers, robbers and witches, do you think you could go to bed by yourself?"

"Yes," said Phoebe smiling an embarrassed little smile, "but I'm awfully hungry. Do you suppose I could have a peanut butter sandwich and a glass of milk?"

"Certainly," said her mother, "but take it upstairs. Now scoot."

So Phoebe scooted. After she had eaten her sandwich and her milk she fell asleep and didn't wake up until she heard Jeremy and Georgie and Chuckie fighting over the catcher's mitt.

At breakfast Georgie said, "Say Phoebe, what was all that bellerin' I heard in your room last night? I never heard so much noise. Screamin' and yellin' and bawlin'. What happened? Did you see your own shadow?"

"I didn't hear anything," said Jeremy. "What was it, a bear?"

Chuckie, who was only three, said, "Oh, bears don't come in houses. Bears live in the woods, don't they, Daddy?"

Phoebe said, "There is nothing that upsets my stummick as much as having to listen to the childish prattle of my brothers. Would you excuse me if I didn't eat my oatmeal, Mother?"

"No, I wouldn't," said her mother, "especially as today is the day of Imogene Haversack's birthday party and you'll probably stuff yourself on candy and ice cream."

"Oh, Imogene's party," said Phoebe, her eyes sparkling. "I had forgotten all about it. May I wear my new pink pique, Mother?"

"I don't see why not," said her mother.

"Oh, Mumsie, can I wear my blue silk?" mocked Georgie. "I do look so pretty in it even if I am the biggest scaredy-cat in the whole United States of America."

"Georgie, eat your cereal and stop teasing," said Mrs. Jackstraw. "More scrambled eggs, Henderson?"

"No thank you, Eloise," said Mr. Jackstraw, his eyes glued to the bad news in the morning paper. "But I would like some coffee."

"It is there right beside you," said Mrs. Jackstraw. "If you would only take your eyes off the paper for a minute you would have seen it."

"I did see it," said Mr. Jackstraw not taking his eyes off the paper as he groped for the sugar bowl. Georgie handed it to him then watched with delight as his father put four teaspoons of sugar in Georgie's cocoa, stirred his own black coffee vigorously, then picked up the cream pitcher and took a sip.

With a splutter he put down his paper for a minute to see what was going on and Mrs. Jackstraw seized this opportunity to say, "Henderson, dear, I must have the car today."

"Sorry," said Mr. Jackstraw, "but I must have it. I have to drive into Greenbrier to interview a witness."

"Oh," said Mrs. Jackstraw. "Well, then Phoebe can take the bus to Imogene's birthday party."

"The bus!" wailed Phoebe. "Oh, Mother, I couldn't. I don't know how."

"What do you mean you don't know how?" said Georgie. "You're not going to steer the bus. You're just going to ride on it."

"Oh, be quiet," Phoebe said. "Mother, please, don't make me take the bus to Imogene's. I won't know where to get off."

"Just tell the driver, dummy," said Jeremy. "That's what I do when I go to Cub Scouts. I just say, 'Let me off at Nickerson Street, driver,' and he does."

"Oh, but that's different," said Phoebe. "You go there every Wednesday. Anyway Imogene lives way over in Blackberry Park."

"So what," Jeremy said. "Mom will tell you what bus to take and where Imogene lives and then you just tell the driver."

"I can't," said Phoebe. "I can't possibly. What if the driver forgot me and I went clear to the end of the line?"

"Get off at Imogene's on the way back," Jeremy said reasonably.

"Well, I'm not going," said Phoebe getting up and throwing her napkin on her chair. "I'm afraid to ride on the bus and I don't care." She stamped out of the dining room.

Putting down his paper, Mr. Jackstraw said, "What's the trouble? Who's afraid of the bus? Where's Phoebe?"

"Oh, that old fraidy-cat has gone up to her room to bawl," said Georgie.

"Gosh, Daddy, she's even afraid to ride on the bus," Jeremy said. "And I been goin' to my Cub Scouts on the bus for ages."

"I rided on the bus once." said Chuckie. "Sarah took me to market with her."

"Really, Henderson," said Mrs. Jackstraw. "Are you positive you have to have the car?"

"Positive," said Mr. Jackstraw. "But if there is something you must have perhaps I can get it for you in Greenbrier. I should be back about four o'clock."

"I don't need anything," said Mrs. Jackstraw, "it is just that I had counted on driving Phoebe to Imogene's birthday party."

"Let her take the bus," said Mr. Jackstraw who hadn't heard one word of the argument.

"But that's the trouble, Daddy," said Jeremy. "She's afraid to take the bus."

Mr. Jackstraw took a sip of coffee, wiped his lips with his napkin, stood up and said, "I'm sure you can handle everything, Eloise. Goodbye boys, say goodbye to Phoebe for me when she gets up."

"But Daddy she's up," said Chuckie.

"Goodbye, son," said Mr. Jackstraw. Then the front door slammed and he was gone.

Jeremy said, "Mom, there's something I been meanin' to ask you, can I have a dog?"

"What kind of a dog?" asked Mrs. Jackstraw.

"A kind of a big black dog that nobody wants," Jeremy said. "He's awful sweet and he's a keen watchdog."

"Where is the dog?" asked his mother. "Does someone have him for sale?"

"Well," said Jeremy. "I just happen to have him right out in the kitchen. The people in the old Haggett house moved away and left him. Do you want to see him?"

"Of course I do," said Mrs. Jackstraw. "Bring him in."

So Jeremy went out in the kitchen and came in leading an enormous black dog which was obviously part

Great Dane. "This is Friendly," he said pushing the dog at his mother. "Sarah and I named him Friendly 'cause he is. Ask him to shake hands, Mom."

Mrs. Jackstraw said, "Shake hands, Friendly!" and Friendly immediately handed her a huge black paw. She shook his paw and he smiled at her. She said, "He's a lovely dog, Jeremy. Are you sure the people left him?"

"We're sure all right," said Sarah, coming in from the kitchen with hot coffee. "The Humane Society man stopped by yesterday and told me all about it. I suggested that we keep him for a while and he was real glad to give him to us. Nobody seems to know what his name is so me and Jeremy named him Friendly."

Georgie said, "He's part mine too, isn't he, Jeremy?"

"He's part all of ours," Jeremy said. "He's our family's dog and I'm going to build him a doghouse."

"That's a fine idea," said Mrs. Jackstraw. "Daddy will help you when he comes home."

Just then Phoebe came into the dining room to tell her mother that she had definitely decided that she would rather stay home from Imogene's party than to take the bus. She got as far as "Mother, I have definitely decided . . ." when she saw Friendly. Giving a shriek she jumped up on a chair and yelled, "Take him out of here! Take that monster out of here."

"That's our new dog, Phoebe, dear," said Mrs. Jackstraw. "His name's Friendly. Shake hands with Phoebe, Friendly."

Friendly walked solemnly over to Phoebe and held out his paw.

She crouched back against the chair and squealed, "Take him away. He's dangerous. He'll bite me!"

"Oh, gosh, what a dope," said Jeremy. "Come here Friendly, ole boy, stay with me and don't go near that big fraidy-cat."

"Motherrrrr," Phoebe wailed, "aren't you going to do anything? Are you going to let that vicious monster stay here?"

"Of course I am," said her mother, "and you are being a very silly little girl. Now get down off that chair and go upstairs and tidy your room."

"Get that dog out of here first," shrieked Phoebe.

"Oh, Mom," said Jeremy. "She's just awful. Come on, Friendly, ole boy, let's go outside."

When Friendly and the three little boys had gone outside and closed the door, Phoebe got down off the dining-room chair, went upstairs and locked herself in her room. She wouldn't come out for lunch, she wouldn't even come out for supper. All she did was snuffle and bawl and say, "I'll never come out of my room as long as you have that dog."

Mrs. Jackstraw talked to her. Mr. Jackstraw talked to her. Sarah talked to her. But it did no good. Finally Mrs. Jackstraw called her friend, Mrs. Melancholy. She said, "Honestly, Bets, I'm at my wit's end. Phoebe is afraid of everything. She is afraid of mice, bugs, dogs, cats, busses, swings, the dark, the light, the water, the mountains. Just everything. Was Shirley ever like that?"

"Not Shirley, but Kathy," said Mrs. Melancholy. "Kathy was even afraid of dolls. She said they might come to life and hurt her. She was also afraid of her bed because she was afraid she might never wake up. But since I sent her to Mrs. Piggle-Wiggle she has been just fine. Last week she won the diving medal at the YWCA. Why don't you call Mrs. Piggle-Wiggle?"

"I will," said Mrs. Jackstraw, "right now. I don't know why I didn't think of her a long time ago. Thanks ever so much, Bets, and tell Kathy I'm awfully proud of her and would love to see her medal."

"And so," said Mrs. Piggle-Wiggle to all of her animals that evening after she had finished milking, "you can see that Phoebe is a very timid child and I shall depend on you all to be as gentle and tame as possible while she is here. That includes you too, Fanny," she said leaning over the trough and poking her with a corn cob, "so wake up and listen."

"Ho, hum," said Fanny heaving to her feet and sending three of her piglets flying into the corner where they landed in a squealing heap.

"I mean it," said Mrs. Piggle-Wiggle. "If I hear so much as one growl out of you, Fanny, I'll put you on a reducing diet of sawdust and hot water."

Sticking out her lower lip and closing her eyes sulkily, Fanny began snuffling around in her trough hoping for a few forgotten crumbs or curds of milk. All she got was a sliver in her snout and a bite on the leg from Armour who was one of the piglets she had knocked into the corner. Feeling very sorry for herself and muttering about what bores visiting children were, she settled down again and went to sleep.

Mrs. Piggle-Wiggle checked the latch on her pen, then she, Lightfoot and Wag started up to the house. They were just under the willow tree when Penelope, with a terrible scream, came hurtling down right on top of them. Mrs. Piggle-Wiggle was so frightened she dropped the basket of eggs and broke five. Wag was so scared he snapped at Lightfoot, and Lightfoot was so surprised she scratched Mrs. Piggle-Wiggle.

"Ho, ho, ho, scared you that time, didn't I?" said Penelope laughing.

"You certainly did," said Mrs. Piggle-Wiggle, "and I don't find it very funny. Especially since I broke five eggs."

"Chickens will lay more," said Penelope. "Dumb old chickens can't do anything but lay eggs. Cackle and lay eggs, that's all chickens are good for. Dumb old chickens can't even talk."

"And that's a blessing," said Mrs. Piggle-Wiggle crossly. "Now, Penelope, I'm having Phoebe Jackstraw out to visit for a while. She's a very timid child and while she's here I do not want you to play any of your scary tricks. I don't want any of that scaring you did tonight. I don't want you to scream like a chicken hawk or hoot like Pulitzer or scream like an eagle. I want you to help Phoebe get over her fraidy-catness."

"I don't know why they call it fraidy-cat," Penelope said. "I don't have much use for cats but they are certainly not afraid."

"Prrrrow," said Lightfoot in assent.

"I don't know where the expression originated," Mrs. Piggle-Wiggle said, "but it has been in use for a long time. Now let's hurry and get supper. Phoebe will be here early tomorrow and I want everything nice and tidy."

Phoebe was at her worst the next morning. She was afraid to have her mother drive. She was afraid her daddy didn't know the way. She was afraid she had forgotten something. She was afraid Mrs. Piggle-Wiggle didn't really want her. When they drove up in front of the farmhouse, Wag was lying quietly on the porch, Lightfoot was curled up on the swing and Penelope was in her cage eating sunflower seeds. But Phoebe wouldn't get out of the car. "I'm afraid," she wailed to her daddy. "Look at all those vicious animals. They'll bite me."

"Oh, what a ninny!" said Penelope softly to Wag.

"She wouldn't even be fun to scare. She'd probably have a fit or faint dead away."

"Please, Phoebe, dear," Mr. Jackstraw was pleading. "If you are afraid of the animals Daddy'll carry you."

Mrs. Piggle-Wiggle said, "Nobody is going to carry a ten-year-old girl into my house. Phoebe, get right out of the car and don't forget your suitcase."

"All right," said Phoebe meekly.

"Now," said Mrs. Piggle-Wiggle to Mr. Jackstraw, "you can run along, Mr. Jackstraw. Phoebe will be just fine."

But Phoebe threw her arms around her daddy's neck and shrieked, "Don't leave me, Daddy. Don't leave me. I'm afraid."

Mrs. Piggle-Wiggle went over and whispered to Penelope. Penelope jumped down to the railing of the porch, and said, "Phoebe Jackstraw, you stop that nonsense right this minute."

Phoebe turned around, saw the green parrot, and said, "Oh, Daddy, look. A parrot and she can talk."

"Why don't you shriek and be afraid of me," said Penelope.

"I don't know," said Phoebe. "Perhaps it is because you can talk."

"Well it's a relief to know that there is something you're not afraid of, anyway," said Penelope. "Even if it has to be me. What in the world ever made you such a ninny, girl?"

"I don't know," said Phoebe. "I'm just afraid of everything."

"Well," said Penelope, "then you'd better live in a cage as I used to. Nothing can get in and you can't get out and you're safe. Everything the same every day. No new experiences. No excitement. You might as well be dead."

"How did you get out of your cage?" asked Phoebe.

"Mrs. Piggle-Wiggle bought me," Penelope said. "The minute she got me out of the pet shop Mrs. Piggle-Wiggle opened the cage door and I rode home on her shoulder. 'Now here is a woman with sense,' I said. Well, let's not stand here talking all day, say goodbye to your daddy. He's got to go to work."

"Goodbye, Daddy," said Phoebe, as calm as a dish of junket.

"Goodbye, Chickabiddy," said her daddy relieved and surprised. "Call me when you are ready to come home."

"I'll call," said Mrs. Piggle-Wiggle. "Goodbye, have a nice day."

"Now," said Mrs. Piggle-Wiggle when the car had gone, "let's go up and put your clothes away. I've given you the small guest room that's right next to my bedroom."

Phoebe's bedroom was very cozy with a sloping ceiling, a high four-poster bed that had a little ladder to climb into it, and a window that looked right into the walnut tree.

"Oh, what a darling room," said Phoebe looking around quickly to see where the light was. There wasn't any. On the bedside table was a candle.

"Do you use candles?" she asked.

"Oh, my yes," said Mrs. Piggle-Wiggle. "Candles and kerosene lamps. When things get better and I sell my apples and walnuts I may buy a light plant."

"Candles make awfully funny shadows," said Phoebe. "Like witches and goblins."

"Not like witches and goblins," said Mrs. Piggle-Wiggle. "Like bunnies and fairies and elves. I can make very good shadow pictures. I'll show you how tonight. Now while you put your clothes away I'm going down in the cellar and get some apples. I thought we'd have applesauce and gingerbread for dessert."

Phoebe carefully laid her clean underclothes and socks and t-shirts in the drawers of the bureau. Then she took her Sunday dress and her coat and started toward the closet. The closet was large and dark. It was under the eaves. Phoebe opened the door and peeked in. Taylor and Philbert, the gray squirrels, who had a secret walnut store in the far corner, thinking she was Mrs. Piggle-Wiggle shouted at her, "Chukka, chukka, chukka."

"Oh, my, oh, goodness," squealed Phoebe slamming the door. "Rats. Big gray rats. Wait till I tell Mrs. Piggle-Wiggle."

Throwing her dress and coat on the bed she ran downstairs calling, "Mrs. Piggle-Wiggle, Mrs. Piggle-Wiggle! Come here quickly. There are rats in my closet."

There was no answer and the kitchen was empty.

Phoebe went out on the back porch. "Mrs. Piggle-Wiggle!" she shouted.

There was no answer.

"Oh, dear," said Phoebe. "She's gone away and left me. What will I do?"

Penelope said, "She has not gone away and left you. I've been here all the time and she hasn't crossed this porch."

"Well, where is she then?" said Phoebe. "I've called and called."

"What were you calling about?" asked Penelope.

"Rats," said Phoebe shuddering. "Huge gray rats in my closet. I was afraid to hang up my dress."

"I'll go up and take a look," said Penelope. "Come along."

"Oh, you go," said Phoebe. "I'm scared to death of rats."

"You're scared to death of everything," said Penelope, "so come along and show me where you saw the rats."

"Oh, all right," said Phoebe. "Do you want to ride on my shoulder?"

"Heavens, no," said Penelope. "I can't abide nervous, jumpy people. I'll walk."

When Phoebe opened the closet door Taylor and Philbert said, "Chukka, chukka, chukka."

Phoebe screamed and Penelope said, "You ninny, those are squirrels. Come here, Taylor and Philbert. Come and show yourselves to this silly girl."

Rolling walnuts ahead of them Taylor and Philbert

came over into the light of the doorway. Phoebe said, "Oh, they are squirrels. Will they bite me?"

"Of course not," said Penelope, "squirrels aren't car-niverous. Thanks boys," she said to the squirrels who sat back expectantly, "she just wanted to see you."

"Now," she said to Phoebe, "hang up your dress and your coat."

Trembling a little, Phoebe did so. Taylor and Phil-bert watched her and as soon as she shut the closet door they went through her coat pockets, took two pieces of salt-water taffy and a stick of Doublemint gum and hid them under the walnuts. When they got down-stairs and Mrs. Piggle-Wiggle still wasn't there Penel-ope suggested that they go down to the barn and look for her.

"Are there animals in the barn?" Phoebe asked fear-fully.

"Naturally," said Penelope, "did you think there'd be Eskimos?"

"Oh, are there Eskimos around here?" said Phoebe shivering.

"No, but Eskimos are very nice people," said Penel-ope. "Now come on."

They walked down to the watering trough. Evelyn and Warren and the goslings and Millard and Martha and the ducklings were swimming around in the pond. Of course the minute he saw Phoebe, Warren began to hiss and stretch his neck and flap his wings. And of course Phoebe screamed and ran back to the house.

"Oh, Warren, for heaven's sake!" Penelope said. "That girl's only a visitor and wouldn't harm your goslings. Anyway, have you forgotten what Mrs. Piggle-Wiggle told us the other night?"

"Whaaaaaaat?" said Warren.

"Whaaaaaaaat, whaaaaaaat?" asked Willard and Martha.

"She told us that this girl Phoebe is very timid and while she is here we are to all be as gentle as possible. Now get back in the pond and hush up. I'll go up to the house and coax her down here again."

So the ducks and the geese got back in the pond and Penelope flew up to the porch and talked Phoebe into coming down to the barn. This time when they went past the watering trough all the ducks and geese sailed around and around smiling at Phoebe and making little ripples in the water.

In the barn there was a great deal of stamping and snorting from Trotsky's stall. "Oh heavens, what is that dreadful noise?" said Phoebe clutching at the ladder to the loft.

"That is Trotsky the horse," said Penelope, "and a gentler, more faithful animal never lived. Let's go in and see him."

"Oh, no," said Phoebe. "Horses are too big."

"Well go up in the loft and look down the hay chute at him," said Penelope.

"Oh, I couldn't," said Phoebe. "I'm afraid of ladders."

"Then," said Penelope sighing, "come around here to the front of his stall. He can't possibly get out and you will have his feed box between you."

So Phoebe timidly crept around to the front of Trot-

sky's stall and Trotsky nodded his head, smiled at her
and put his nose down to be stroked.

Instead of stroking his nose, Phoebe jumped as if he
had bitten her. "Get back, get back," she shrieked.

Trotsky looked at Penelope in a very bewildered way.
Penelope said, "You'll just have to excuse her, Trotsky,
she's more timid than a wild rabbit. Say, how come
you're all saddled and bridled?"

Trotsky shrugged his shoulders.

"Come on Phoebe," Penelope said, "I'll show you
Fanny and the piglets, Clematis and the lambs, Heather
and Arbutus, the bunnies and the chickens, the turkeys
and their poults and Georgette, Layette and Paulette and their baby chicks. I can tell right now that you
won't want to see Pulitzer the owl or Billy the Bat or
Winston Toad."

Fanny was fairly civil to Phoebe, and the piglets
were darling. They squealed and played and when
Penelope pulled up the little door into Lester's pen,
Armour and Swift came in and let Phoebe hold them
and pat them.

Heather was as timid and sweet smelling as any little
calf and Phoebe hugged her around the neck and
scratched her behind the ears.

Clematis and the lambs wouldn't come up to the pasture fence but Phoebe got to see them and she thought
Clematis had let herself go terribly and the lambs were
just like toys. Of course Phoebe was scared to death of
Tom and Tomara and jumped ten feet in the air when
Tom gobbled at her. She didn't mind the chickens so
much but her hands were so trembly when she gathered

the eggs she cracked three on the edge of the nests. She
liked the bunnies but she was afraid of the old hens who
were taking dust baths in the sunshine by the manure
pile.

"Well, that's that," said Penelope when the tour was
over. "Now we'd better go up and ask Mrs. Piggle-
Wiggle why Trotsky is saddled. It may be that she is
going to teach you to ride."

"Oh, no, please not that," said Phoebe shivering. "I
don't want to ride. I wouldn't know how to steer."

"Even I can steer Trotsky," said Penelope. "You just
tell him where you want to go and he goes. When you
get there he stops. If you want to stop before he does
you say, Whoa. Now isn't that easy?"

"What if I fall off?" said Phoebe.

"Why should you fall off?" said Penelope. "Anyway,
you've got stirrups to put your feet in and the saddle
horn to hold on to. Now let's get up to the house."

When they got up to the house they still didn't see
Mrs. Piggle-Wiggle. She wasn't upstairs, she wasn't in
the parlor, she wasn't in the kitchen. "Did she tell you
where she was going?" asked Penelope.

"No," said Phoebe, "I mean yes, she did. She said
she was going to the cellar to get some apples."

"Well, maybe we'd better look in the cellar then,"
said Penelope. "The door is outside there under the
dining-room window."

One of the doors was open but it was pretty dark
down in the cellar so Penelope sent Phoebe to the
kitchen for a candle and some matches. Phoebe said
that she was afraid of matches but Penelope said, "Let's

have none of that nonsense, girl. Strike a match and be quick about it, I'm worried about Mrs. Piggle-Wiggle."

So Phoebe struck the match and lit the candle and she and Penelope went into the cellar. They found Mrs. Piggle-Wiggle in the fruit closet with a barrel of apples on her foot. She was faint with pain and her voice was just a whisper as she said, "You won't be able to move the apples, Phoebe. Get on Trotsky and ride as fast as you can over to Larsens' and send Nels back to move this barrel. Penelope, you go upstairs and call the doctor. Just tell the operator to get him for you. Everybody hurry please, I'm in great pain." She closed her eyes.

Penelope jumped on Phoebe's shoulder and said, "Come on girl, run. Run as fast as you can down to the barn."

So Phoebe ran and when she got to the barn, Penelope told her to untie Trotsky and lead him to the watering trough. Then she told her to climb up on the watering trough and then up on to Trotsky's back. "Now put your feet in the stirrups," she said when Phoebe was in the saddle, "pick up the reins. All right, Trotsky, take her over to Larsens' as fast as you can. Hang on tight, Phoebe, but don't slow down."

At first Phoebe was so scared she closed her eyes and lay forward in the saddle like a sack of corn meal. Trotsky didn't gallop which is very joggly and hard on a new rider, but ran using his right hind foot and left forefoot together and his left hind foot and right forefoot together. There was so little motion that the first thing Phoebe knew she was sitting up and holding on to the reins and loving riding horseback. The wind blew in her mouth, the fences streaked by in long lines and the trees looked like fences. Then they were in the Larsens' lane, then in their barnyard and Mr. Larsen came running up from the tractor shed. "What's the matter?" he said. "I saw you clear over by the oat field. Who are you?"

"I'm Phoebe Jackstraw," said Phoebe, "and Mrs. Piggle-Wiggle's hurt. A barrel of apples fell on her foot and she can't get it off. She wants you quick."

"Move up," said Nels vaulting into the saddle behind her. "All right Trotsky, go!" He put one strong arm around Phoebe and Trotsky galloped all the way

home. Galloping was like being in a boat in a storm Phoebe thought. Up and then slap down hard, up again and then slap down again. Phoebe loved it but she was glad Nels held her on.

When they got to the farm Penelope was waiting on the porch. She said, "You certainly made good time. The doctor's on his way." She flew to Nels' shoulder. "The cellar's over this way," she said. "Phoebe, go in and build the kitchen fire and put some water on to heat. You might make a pot of coffee while you're at it." She and Nels went around the house.

Phoebe went into the kitchen. She had never made a fire in her life and the only stove she had ever seen was her mother's electric range. She wished Penelope had stayed to help her. She opened the little door in the front of the stove. The firebox was black. No coals even. In the woodbox there was some kindling. A newspaper in the rocking chair. Rumpling up the newspaper Phoebe stuffed it in the stove, and poked in some of the smallest pieces of kindling. Then she lit a match. To her amazement the paper flared up and caught the kindling. When the kindling began to crackle Phoebe poked in some bigger sticks. They soon caught and began to burn too. She was so proud she kept opening the little door and peering in at her fire. She almost forgot about the water. She lifted the kettle. It was empty. Carrying it to the back porch she set it down in front of the pump and fearfully lifted the handle of the pump. There was a loud slurping sound like somebody getting the last drop out of an ice-cream soda. With a frightened gasp Phoebe dropped the pump handle. "My gosh this thing is going to explode," she said to Wag, who was watching her. "I think I'd better go down by the pond."

Barking, Wag jumped up and with both paws pulled down the pump handle. A small stream of water came out of the mouth of the pump into the tea kettle. "Is that the way you do it?" Phoebe asked Wag. Wag barked. So Phoebe gingerly lifted up the pump handle again, it made the same gurgling noise until she pushed down on it and then a stream of water as big as her thumb came out. She pumped again and more water came out. So she pumped until she had the kettle full. "Say, pumping's fun," she said to Wag as she lifted up the full kettle and put it on the stove.

Her fire was going very well now but she poked in wood until the firebox was clear full. Penelope came into the kitchen. "Did you get the fire going all right?" she asked.

"See," said Phoebe opening the firebox door.

"Looks fine," said Penelope, "did you open the draught?"

"What's that?" asked Phoebe.

"That little thing on the side," said Penelope. "See those little windows? Well they should all be opened or closed, I forget which."

"They're closed now, so I'll open them," said Phoebe. She did and the fire roared. "This is fun," she told Penelope. "And I pumped water too, Wag showed me how."

"Fine, fine," said Penelope, "now, what about coffee? How do you make that?"

"I don't know," said Phoebe. "I don't even know where Mrs. Piggle-Wiggle keeps it."

"It's in the pantry in a red can," said Penelope. "All you do is put some in the coffee pot, pour in some water, put in an eggshell and let it boil."

"But how much coffee and how much water do you use?" asked Phoebe.

"Fill er up," said Penelope.

"I'm going to look on the can," said Phoebe. "Here it is. It says, 'one tablespoon of coffee for each cup of water.' That's easy."

103

When Nels carried Mrs. Piggle-Wiggle into the kitchen a few minutes later, the fire was snapping, the kettle was humming and the coffee pot was on.

Nels put Mrs. Piggle-Wiggle in the rocker by the stove and she said, "Everything is so cosy I feel better already."

When the doctor came he said nothing was broken but he bandaged Mrs. Piggle-Wiggle's foot and told her to keep off it for a day or so. Then he and Mrs. Piggle-Wiggle and Nels had a cup of coffee and some sugar cookies.

When he was ready to leave he said, "You're mighty fortunate to have this fine, brave, girl to help you, Mrs. Piggle-Wiggle. Poor old Mrs. Findock was all alone when she hurt her foot last winter and so of course she had to walk on it too soon and it took much longer to heal."

Mrs. Piggle-Wiggle said, "I know how lucky I am. Imagine having a visitor who can ride horseback, make fires, pump water, and cook. Now all I have to worry about is the milking."

"I'll milk for you," said Nels.

"I'll help you," said Phoebe. "I already know how to gather eggs."

"Okay," said Nels, "but first I'd better teach you how to unsaddle and feed Trotsky."

"Before you do either of those things, I'd like to ask a favor," said Mrs. Piggle-Wiggle. "Would someone please go down in the cellar and get me those apples. I can peel them while I'm resting my foot."

"I'll go," said Nels.

"No, let me," said Phoebe picking up the apple pan and running out the door.

"Wait," called Mrs. Piggle-Wiggle. "It's dark down there. You'll need a candle."

But Phoebe apparently didn't hear her because she didn't wait. In a minute she was back in the kitchen with cobwebs in her hair and a big pan of red apples in her arms.

"Good girl," said Nels. "Now let's go down and take care of the animals."

When they had gone, Penelope jumped on Mrs. Piggle-Wiggle's lap, took a bite of her sugar cookie and a sip of her coffee and said, "You know, Mrs. Piggle-Wiggle, when Phoebe first came here, I thought she was the worst ninny I had ever seen and I could hardly wait for her to go home. Now I wish she'd stay all summer."

"So do I," said Mrs. Piggle-Wiggle.

# V. THE CAN'T FIND IT CURE

"Morton, dear," said Mrs. Heatherwick, "would you please run upstairs and get me my gold thimble. It is in my workbasket and the workbasket is on the little table by the window."

"Okay," said Morton cheerfully putting down his paintbrush right in the middle of painting a picture of a cowboy roping a wild steer. He went up the stairs two at a time and was in his mother's bedroom in four seconds. As soon as he got inside the room, however, his energy seemed to disappear and he stood limply gazing like a puppet up at the ceiling. After he had looked at the ceiling for a while he looked out the window.

"Gee, this window has a good view," Morton said as he gazed over the countryside. He could see Mr. Johnson clipping tent caterpillars off his apple trees. He could see Mrs. Greer setting out petunias. He could see Jody Jones sitting on his bed not cleaning up his room. He could see Sharon Rogers doing figure eights on her roller skates on Willow Street. "If a person stayed up by this ole window long enough," Morton said, "he could learn about everything that is going on in the whole world."

Then up the stairs floated his mother's voice, "Morton," she called. "What in the world are you doing? Bring me my thimble."

Morton went downstairs and said, "I couldn't find it."

"Did you look in my workbasket?" asked his mother.

"What workbasket," said Morton.

"The one on the table by the window," said his mother.

"Oh, that one," said Morton as if his mother's room was a solid mass of workbaskets.

"Now go up and get me my thimble," said his mother impatiently. "I can't poke this needle through your jeans without it and I have four pairs to patch."

So Morton went upstairs again. This time his dog,

Tagalong, met him at the top of the stairs, licked his face and told him very plainly that something was wrong with him.

"What is it, ole boy?" said Morton hugging Tagalong. "What's the trouble?"

"Mmmmmmm, owwwwwwww, mmmmm," said Tagalong holding up his paw, and showing Morton the burr that was in between his toes.

"Oh, you poor old boy," said Morton. "Here hold still and I'll get it out for you. There now isn't that better?"

Tagalong said it wasn't so Morton looked and saw that he had burrs all over him.

"Well," said Morton going in and getting his mother's silver backed hairbrush and comb. "We'll just comb all those mean ole burrs out, won't we, boy?"

Half an hour later, Mrs. Heatherwick came to the foot of the stairs and called, "Morton, where is that thimble?"

"Oh, that," said Morton. "I couldn't find it."

With a sigh of exasperation his mother ran upstairs, went into her bedroom, opened her workbasket on the little table by the window and saw that the gold thimble was there in plain sight. She then went out into the hall, took Morton by the ear, led him in and showed him the thimble. He said, "Well, my gosh, you mean in that workbasket."

His mother said, "Is that my silver hairbrush you are holding?"

"I guess so," said Morton.

"What are you doing with it?" said his mother.

"Just taking burrs out of ole Tagalong," said Morton.

"Brushing a dog with my silver hairbrush!" shrieked his mother.

"Well, yes," said Morton. "It's better than mine for burrs because it has stiffer bristles."

"And I suppose you used my comb too," said his mother.

"I tried to," said Morton, "but it pulls Tagalong's fur and he doesn't like it."

"Morton Heatherwick," said his mother, "you go right out and get me my comb and don't let me, ever as long as I live, find you using it again for anything."

So Morton went out in the hall and called back, "I can't find it."

"You can't find it?" said his mother. "That's ridiculous. You were just using it."

"But it isn't here," said Morton. "Somebody's taken it."

"And who would take it?" said his mother.

"I don't know," said Morton, "but somebody sure did. A cat burglar maybe. They can come in a house and you can't hear 'em at all."

"If a cat burglar came in this house Tagalong would bark," said Mrs. Heatherwick. "Anyway what would a cat burglar want with a comb with two broken teeth filled with dog hairs and burrs."

"I don't know," said Morton, "but sometimes those burglars are kind of crazy and take anything."

"There has been no cat burglar in this house," said Mrs. Heatherwick in a very exasperated voice. "There never has been a cat burglar in this house and there never will be a cat burglar in this house. NOW FIND MY COMB!"

Just then Tagalong got up to go after a fly that was buzzing on the hall window and there on the floor where he had been lying was the comb.

"Hey, Mom, here's your comb," said Morton picking it up and handing it to her with a proud smile. "It was layin' right there on the floor, under ole Tagalong."

"It is ly-ing," said his mother. "Now if you want to continue to take burrs out of Tagalong go down in the basement and get his comb and brush. They are on the shelf above the wash tubs, right next to his flea powder and the worm medicine."

"Oh, I know," said Morton. "Come on Tagalong, ole boy. We'll get out those old burrs." They ran down the stairs and his mother could hear Morton clumping down into the basement.

In two seconds a shout came up the basement stairs, "Hey, Mom, I can't find Tagalong's brush. It isn't on that shelf."

"It is too," shouted back his mother. "I saw it yesterday. It is right above the wash tubs."

So Morton looked on the gardening shelf by the door and couldn't find Tagalong's brush and comb but he did see a can of paint he had bought the summer before for his bicycle. "Say, that's what I wanted to do today," he said to Tagalong. "Paint my bike. I'm gonna paint her bright red with silver trimmings. Boy, ole Benji Franklin will be jealous. His bike's as rusty as a tin can. Come on Tag, let's wheel the bike over here under the window so we can see what we are doing."

At lunch time, when Morton came upstairs his mother said, "Did you get the burrs off Tagalong?"

"Oh, I couldn't find the brush and comb," Morton said, "but I been paintin' my bike. It looks swell."

"Did you put newspapers on the floor first?" asked his mother.

"No," said Morton. "But I'm only paintin' the top part right now."

"Have you spilled any paint?" asked his mother.

"Oh, a little," said Morton, "but I wiped it up, see?" He held up his handkerchief which looked as if he had had a bad nosebleed.

"Not your handkerchief?" wailed his mother.

"Sure," said Morton, "and I got every drop of paint off the floor."

"Well," said Mrs. Heatherwick, "from now on use an old rag to wipe up the paint and *please* spread newspapers all over the floor where you are painting. There is a bottle of turpentine in the paint cupboard. Put a little on this old rag and take the paint off your face, out of your hair and off your arm."

"Sure, Mom," said Morton. "I will, as soon as I finish this banana."

But of course when Morton finished his banana he couldn't find the turpentine.

"Mom, where'd you say that turpentine is?" he yelled from the basement. "I looked in the fruit cupboard. And it isn't there."

"I didn't say it was in the fruit cupboard," his mother said. "I told you it was in the paint cupboard. It is on the top shelf."

"It isn't there," he yelled a few minutes later, but fortunately Mrs. Heatherwick was up changing her clothes to go to her ceramics class and couldn't hear him. When she was dressed she told Morton to go over to Mrs. Beecham's and play with Enterprise while she was gone.

He said, "Aw, Mom, I hate to go to Beechams'. Mrs. Beecham is so darned clean she makes us look at television through the window and she won't let Tagalong on her property."

"Then why don't you ask Enterprise over here," Mrs. Heatherwick said. "You could play croquet."

"Oh, we can't play croquet," Morton said, "I can't find any of the balls."

"They are in the garage," said his mother.

"Oh, no they aren't, Mom," Morton said. "I looked yesterday."

So Mrs. Heatherwick said, "Well, why don't you and Enterprise make popcorn then. The electric popper is in the pan cupboard."

"Oh, I love popcorn," Morton said. "That's a swell idea, Mom. Goodbye, have a good time."

Mrs. Heatherwick went out to the garage and got in the car. As she backed out she noticed the croquet balls in a neat row on Mr. Heatherwick's work bench. She sighed and wondered if Morton was going blind.

Mrs. Heatherwick usually loved her ceramics class. All of her very best friends attended and they made so many lovely things. Ash trays with roses on them. Plates with roses on them. Bowls with roses on them. Cigarette boxes with roses on them. Even napkin rings, spoon holders and match boxes with roses on them. But today was to be the climax of the whole wonderful course. They were going to make just roses. Great big life-size roses not attached to anything. Not to be used for anything but to be put around the house in artistic places. On the radio for instance, or on the telephone table or on the mantel. Places like that. A real ceramic rose would be beautiful anywhere Mrs. Heatherwick thought. She hummed a happy little tune as she molded her rose. The telephone rang. It was Morton for her. He said, "Where is the popcorn, Mom?"

She said, "In the cupboard with the cereals."

She went back to her rose which was beginning to look less and less like a mildewed cabbage. The telephone rang again. It was for Mrs. Heatherwick. Morton said, "I can't find the popcorn, Mom."

She said, "It is right next to the Shredded Wheat and beside the Sugar Pops. You can't miss it."

She went back to her rose. The telephone rang. It was Morton. He said, "I can't find the popcorn popper."

She said, "I told you it was in the pan cupboard. It is on the top shelf at the back. Plug it in to the outlet on the stove. The popcorn was right where I told you, wasn't it?"

Morton said, "Oh, I couldn't find our popcorn so Enterprise went home and got his. Well, 'bye, Mom."

That was the last call and so Mrs. Heatherwick presumed that Morton had found the popper. She put a bright pink glaze on her rose and was very proud of the real little thorns she had made. Lou Hopscotch told her it was the prettiest rose in the whole class and she would bake it in her kiln and it would be ready to take home and put on her radio by Saturday. Mrs. Heatherwick was as happy as a bee.

When she got home the very first thing she was going to do was to go in the living room and decide where the beautiful rose would look the best. But when she got home and went into the living room she gave a scream and put her hands over her eyes. What appeared to be two black faced old trappers were crouched over a smoking fire in the fireplace shaking a greasy skillet. All around them in every direction was an inch deep carpet of greasy burned popcorn and salt. "What in the world are you doing?" shrieked Mrs. Heatherwick.

"Makin' popcorn," said the voice of Morton from the face of the blackest trapper. "We couldn't find the electric popper so we built a fire in the fireplace and we're doing it the old-fashioned way."

"Take it out of here right now," said Mrs. Heatherwick grimly, "and bring me the vacuum cleaner."

"Gosh, Morton, I gotta go home," Enterprise said edging toward the door.

"You are staying until this mess is cleaned up," said Mrs. Heatherwick.

"Well, all right," said Enterprise taking the hearthbroom and swacking at the popcorn so that a piece hit Mrs. Heatherwick in the eye.

"Oh, go on home," she said. "And you, Morton, go up to your room. I'll clean this up, it's safer."

It took her about an hour to vacuum up all the popcorn, about three hours to get the grease stains off her new gray carpet, and about two seconds to find the electric corn popper exactly where she had told Morton it was.

When Mr. Heatherwick came home, starving and hoping for an apple pie or maybe a hot fresh chocolate cake, he found his wife bawling in the kitchen. She said, "This is the worst day I have ever had and I'm sure Morton is going blind."

"Oh, my gosh, how awful," said Mr. Heatherwick. "Where is he?"

"Up in his room," said Mrs. Heatherwick.

So Mr. Heatherwick tore upstairs and burst in on Morton who was carefully finishing his painting of a cowboy roping a wild steer. "Hi, Dad," he said not looking up.

"Oh, son," said Mr. Heatherwick, "that's a wonderful painting. How do you do it? Do you feel around with your fingers?"

"Course not," said Morton. "I just look at it and paint."

"Look at it?" said Mr. Heatherwick. "Can you see?"

"Of course I can see," said Morton. "I've got the best eyesight in our room at school. The nurse said so."

So Mr. Heatherwick went downstairs and told Mrs. Heatherwick that Morton had the best eyesight in school and Mrs. Heatherwick told him about the thimble and the comb and Tagalong's brush and comb and the turpentine and the popcorn and the popcorn popper and the croquet balls.

"Well," Mr. Heatherwick said, "let's see if he can find a switch."

"Oh, not that," said Mrs. Heatherwick. "Not physical punishment, Justin. There must be a better way."

"What about Mrs. Piggle-Wiggle, then?" said Mr. Heatherwick.

"That's it," said Mrs. Heatherwick. "That's the answer. I'll call her right now."

Friday morning just when Morton was due to arrive, Nels Larsen came galloping up on Charlie, his old white horse, and told Mrs. Piggle-Wiggle that he had seen a huge coyote in his wheat field. "He's after something," he said. "Has Arbutus had her calf?"

"I don't think so," said Mrs. Piggle-Wiggle. "I tried to bring her in the barn last night to give her some hay but she wouldn't come. She didn't have any calf with her though. I watched her for some time. She is in that middle section of pasture, the one with the stream running through it."

"Well," said Nels. "If I were you, I'd keep an eye on her. You know how cows are about hiding their calves. If she wouldn't come in the barn last night the chances are she has had her calf and is hiding it. That old coyote knows it, too. As soon as I saw him I went up to the house and got my gun but of course he'd gone when I got back. They're the sneakiest animals there are."

Just then Morton's father drove up and delivered Morton. "I am certainly glad to see you," said Mrs. Piggle-Wiggle hugging Morton. "I need somebody with sharper eyes and faster legs than mine."

"Why," asked Morton stroking Charlie's nose.

"Because Mr. Larsen here, saw a coyote in his wheat field and we think Arbutus has had her calf and hidden it. If the coyote finds it before we do he'll kill it."

"Don't worry, Mrs. Piggle-Wiggle, I'll find that ole calf for you," Morton said. "Well, goodbye, Dad, I got work to do."

"Goodbye, son," said Mr. Heatherwick. "Be good and help Mrs. Piggle-Wiggle all you can."

"Of course I will," said Morton dropping his suitcase, his box of games, his bow and arrow, his paintbox and his drawing paper in a heap by the back steps. Then stripping off his jacket and throwing it on top of the other things he said, "Now where did you say this ole calf might be, Mrs. Piggle-Wiggle?"

"Here, get up here with me," said Nels reaching down for Morton's hands. "I'll ride you over and show you."

"Yipes!" said Morton when he was astride the horse in front of Nels. "Say, Dad, look at me. I'm riding horseback just like a cowboy."

"Giddap," said Nels and Charlie slowly meandered off in the direction of the wheat field.

After he had shown Morton where the coyote had been Nels took him to the middle pasture where Arbutus was. They got off Charlie and walked over to Arbutus who was over by the north fence eating clover.

"Hi, old girl," said Nels slapping her on the side. Arbutus blinked her eyes and chewed her clover.

Morton said, "Gosh, she's pretty. Do you think I can learn to milk her?"

"Of course," said Nels. "But first you'd better find her calf. When you do find it let me know and I'll carry it up to the barn."

Then Nels rode away on Charlie and Morton sat down in the clover by Arbutus and thought about the calf. "I'd like to have a little calf of my very own," he thought. "I'd have it sleep with me and take it to school with me just like a dog. I'd name it Pal and when it grew up and was a big dangerous bull I'd ride it in a rodeo."

While Morton was busy with these thoughts Arbutus lay down and began to chew her cud. Morton thought this was nice and friendly of her. He said, "You're a nice old girl, Arbutus and I won't let any old coyote get your calf. I'll find it and then we'll put it in the barn where it will be safe." Arbutus closed her eyes.

While he had been talking Morton had been running his fingers through the clover. He felt something round and kind of soft. He looked down and saw that he had a fat red wild strawberry in his hand. He put it in his mouth. It was warm and sweet and delicious. "Oh, boy," said Morton. "Wild strawberries, I'll bring some back to Mrs. Piggle-Wiggle." Crawling on his hands and knees he began to pick the little strawberries and put them in his handkerchief. He had about a cupful when he looked up and saw a small brown rabbit watching him. "Hi, bunny," he said sitting back on his heels

and absent-mindedly putting a handful of the strawberries in his mouth. The bunny hopped away. Morton followed him. Then the bunny disappeared down a hole near a log. Morton put his hand way down the hole but he couldn't feel anything but dirt. He was quite disappointed and rather tired so he lay down on the grass on his back and looked at the sky.

A big chicken hawk was flying around in the clear spring sky. He moved slowly, surely in big circles. Then a meadow lark began to sing. He stood on a fence post and tossed his song into the air. The clear sweet notes floated around in the sunshine like soap bubbles. A beetle as shiny and black as licorice crawled over

Morton's fingers and went charging into the deep grass. "I sure like to live in the country," said Morton. "I guess I'll go down to that stream and find a willow tree. I feel like making a willow whistle."

So he went down to the stream and he found a willow tree and he also found a big green frog, a little yellow water snake, two crickets, and a handful of periwinkles. He put the periwinkles in his handkerchief with the rather squashed strawberries. He put the green frog inside his shirt. He put the crickets in his back pocket and he carried the snake. "Boy, Mrs. Piggle-Wiggle will be glad," he said as he ambled across the pasture toward home.

Of course when he tried to go under the fence the crickets got away. He chased them for a while and finally gave up. The sun was pretty hot and anyway there were lots of crickets. He sat down in the shade of a maple tree and took out Pal, his frog. He had forgotten all about Pal, the little calf he was going to find. Pal the frog was a beautiful shade of green with a yellow stomach. He swelled up his throat and blinked his eyes at Morton. Morton said, "When we get home I'll make you a little bed out of a matchbox and you can sleep in my room. I'll catch flies for you and you can swim in the watering trough."

Pal said, "Currrunk."

My, but it was peaceful there under the maple tree! Morton closed his eyes. A little breeze riffled through his hair. He fell asleep. When he woke up it was afternoon. Pal was gone and he was very hungry. Grabbing up the handkerchief with the periwinkles and squashed strawberries in it, he ran across the field, over the hill, through the little woods, up by the barn and on to Mrs. Piggle-Wiggle's back porch. She was in the kitchen baking peanut butter cookies. "Oh, Morton," she said, "you wonderful boy! You found the calf! I knew you would."

"The calf?" Morton said, taking six of the hot peanut butter cookies and cramming three into his mouth. "What calf?"

"Arbutus' calf that she had hidden," Mrs. Piggle-Wiggle said. "You went out to look for her hours ago."

"Oh, that calf," said Morton. "I couldn't find it. But I brought you some wild strawberries." He opened his handkerchief and showed Mrs. Piggle-Wiggle the strawberries all smashed and mixed in with the periwinkles.

She said, "Ugh."

"They don't look very good, do they?" Morton said. "I guess I must have sat on them, or something." He took six more cookies.

"Where did you look for the calf?" asked Mrs. Piggle-Wiggle.

"Oh, around in the grass," Morton said. "He wasn't anywhere."

"Did you look down by the stream?" asked Mrs. Piggle-Wiggle.

"Yeah," said Morton, "and I found a swell little frog. I named him Pal and he had a yellow stomach. Gee, he was cute. He ran away though when I fell asleep."

"Asleep!" said Mrs. Piggle-Wiggle. "You mean

you've been sleeping while Arbutus' poor little calf is lying out in the field prey for that horrible coyote?"

"I was kind of tired from picking all those strawberries and so I just took a little nap," Morton said reaching for more cookies.

Mrs. Piggle-Wiggle looked at the dozen or so strawberries and then at Morton. She said, "I am very very disappointed in you, Morton. You haven't been looking for the calf at all and the sun is going down and pretty soon it will be night and the coyote will come sneaking down from the hills and find the little calf and kill it. You should be ashamed of yourself. Very ashamed. Apparently you don't love animals at all."

"I do too," said Morton. "I was going to find that ole calf and name him Pal and raise him up to a big bull and everything, but then I saw those strawberries and then I chased a rabbit and then I chased some crickets."

"Well," said Mrs. Piggle-Wiggle, "you'd better come down to the barn and help me with the chores so I can go out and look for the calf."

Morton was not too much help with the chores. He couldn't find the pitchfork to pitch down hay for Trotsky. He couldn't find the calf meal for Heather. He couldn't find the oats for Trotsky, and when Mrs. Piggle-Wiggle sent him up to the house to get the bucket of slops for Fanny, he came back with a crock of cherry-leaf pickles and another handful of cookies. Exasperated Mrs. Piggle-Wiggle said, "Go up and stay in your room. You are no help at all. *I* will finish the chores and then *I* will find the calf."

Morton's feelings were very hurt and he thought Mrs. Piggle-Wiggle was being unnecessarily cross. He shuffled up to the house, dragged up to his room and slumped down on the bed. "Mrs. Piggle-Wiggle doesn't like me, that's the trouble," he said to Lightfoot who was asleep on his pillow. "Nobody likes me. Mom and Dad sent me out here to get rid of me and now Mrs. Piggle-Wiggle wants to get rid of me. She'll probably send me to a orphan asylum. And I didn't even have any lunch." He began to cry.

Wag who had followed him up to the house licked his hand and whimpered. He hated to see anyone feel sad. Wiping his eyes on his sleeve, Morton said, "Well,

I guess as long as nobody likes me or wants me I'd better run away. I'll go up to Alaska and dig gold and
when I'm rich I'll came back and I won't speak to any
of them, will I, Wag?"

Wag wagged his tail and smiled and Morton got up
off the bed and ran away.

He ran down the lane, through the little woods and
down into the field where he had been picking the wild
strawberries. When he got in the field he decided that
he might as well look for Pal, his frog. He went over
to the place under the maple tree where he had been
asleep earlier in the day. My, but it was dark and
gloomy there now. The sun had gone down and the
shadows were as black as caves. "I'll never be able to
see old Pal here," Morton said to Wag. "Anyway he's
probably gone back to the brook. Let's go down there."

It was pretty dark down by the brook too. Dark and
wet. Morton stepped on what he thought was a hum-
mock of grass and went clear to his knee in water.
When he pulled his foot out it made a very unpleasant
sucking sound. "Quicksand!" he said to Wag. "We'd
better get out of here quick." So they went back across
the field to the maple tree, and sat down. All around
them were strange night sounds. Rustlings in the leaves,
snapping of twigs, chirping of frogs, cries of night
hawks, the mournful too-whoo of Pulitzer. Morton
shivered and put his arm around Wag. He wished he
were in Mrs. Piggle-Wiggle's cozy kitchen. Then from
across the valley the coyote howled. It was a terrible
sound. Fierce and lonely and wild. Jumping up Morton said to Wag, "I'm going to climb up in this old

maple tree and sleep. That's what hunters do. You can come up too if you want, Wag."

Wag barked.

So Morton climbed in the tree. High up. In fact so high up he could see for about a hundred miles. He could see the lights at the Larsens' farm. He could see the stream winding through the valley, he could see the old bee tree up behind Mrs. Piggle-Wiggle's house, he could even see Arbutus down in the field. She was bending down eating. No, she wasn't, she was licking something, and she was kind of mooing. Maybe it was the calf.

"Zowie!" Morton shinnied down out of the tree quicker than a squirrel and ran as fast as he could over to the far corner of the field, down by the stream where Arbutus was. The minute she saw him Arbutus started to walk away, but Morton had marked the place where she had been by a wild cherry tree. He went right to the tree and there, curled up in some rushes, hidden by young willows, was a little brown and white calf. Morton knelt down and patted it. He said, "I found you and you're mine, little Pal. You look like a baby deer."

Then from just across the creek came the cry of the coyote, Arbutus bellowed. Wag barked and Morton stood up and shouted, "Mrs. Piggle-Wiggle, I found him. I found him."

Mrs. Piggle-Wiggle called out, "Stay there, I'm coming."

Her barn lantern bobbed along through the field like a firefly. Morton was glad she brought it. "That old coyote sounded awful close."

Mrs. Piggle-Wiggle said, "Oh, Morton, you brave boy to wait in the dark until Arbutus led you to her calf. I certainly misjudged you and I'm certainly sorry."

Morton said, "Oh, that's all right, Mrs. Piggle-Wiggle. Now you stay here while I go and get Nels. Come on, Wag."

Nels carried the little calf up to the barn and Arbutus followed. When they had them nice and cozy in a box stall, Mrs. Piggle-Wiggle said, "Because you are such a brave boy, Morton, and such a wonderful finder, I'm going to give you this little calf. What do you want to name her?"

"Her?" said Morton. "I wanted a little bull."

"Well, you have a fine little heifer," said Nels.

"Well, then I'll name her Wild Strawberry," said Morton.

"That's a beautiful name," said Mrs. Piggle-Wiggle, "I couldn't have picked a better one myself. Now what would you say to some supper?"

"Oh, boy," said Morton.

"I've baked beans and made brown bread and I think there's a cherry pie in the pantry."

It was truly remarkable how finding the lost calf changed Morton Heatherwick. The very next morning when Mrs. Piggle-Wiggle asked him if he would pitch down some hay for Trotsky, instead of ambling up the ladder, flopping down in the hay, staring up at Billy the Bat hanging upside down from a rafter and then yelling down at Mrs. Piggle-Wiggle "I can't find the pitchfork," he ran up the ladder, found the pitchfork right away, and pitched down the hay.

Then when he was putting the pitchfork away, over by the window, hidden by a box, he found Mrs. Henry, the Plymouth Rock hen Mrs. Nelson had given Mrs. Piggle-Wiggle. Mrs. Henry was sitting on a nest of sixteen big brown eggs. Mrs. Piggle-Wiggle was perfectly delighted. Mrs. Henry had been missing for days and she was afraid a weasel had gotten her. Morton took Mrs. Henry a dish of water and some grain and she clucked at him.

That same afternoon after lunch when Morton was away high up in the walnut tree putting up a swing he saw Lightfoot come out of the cellar with a kitten in her mouth. Holding her head high so the fat kitten wouldn't drag she ran across the back yard and into the woodshed. In a few minutes she went back to the cellar and got another kitten. And another and another.

Morton could hardly wait to tell Mrs. Piggle-Wiggle. He slid down the swing rope so fast his hands burned, and raced into the kitchen. "Mrs. Piggle-Wiggle," he said, "Lightfoot has four kittens, and I know where she's got them hidden."

Every single day he found something—the mallard duck's nest, two horseshoes, a bee tree, a rusty sledge hammer, an Indian arrowhead and Mrs. Piggle-Wiggle's cameo brooch that had been lost for two months. He found that under the mash hopper in the chicken house. He put it in the egg basket and when Mrs. Piggle-Wiggle saw it she got tears in her eyes. She lifted it out very gently, washed it under the pump, pinned it on her dress, and said, "That was the very first present Mr. Piggle-Wiggle gave me. It means more to me than anything. Thank you from the bottom of my heart, Morton."

Morton said, "Aw, it wasn't anything, Mrs. Piggle-Wiggle. I just happen to have much sharper eyes than anybody in the whole world." He jumped off the porch and shinnied up the walnut tree.

# ABOUT THE AUTHOR

BETTY MACDONALD was born in Boulder, Colorado, and grew up in various places in the West. As a child her activities included singing, ballet, piano, French, dramatics, cooking, shooting, and roof-painting. She attended Roosevelt High School in Seattle and the University of Washington.

Ms. MacDonald worked at an assortment of jobs: as secretary to a mining engineer, tinting photographs, keeping records for a rabbit grower, running a chain letter office, modeling fur coats, and selling advertising. She also did government work, which included teaching art and writing.

She was married twice, first to a chicken farmer named Robert Haskett (her successful book THE EGG AND I was based on reminiscences of their experiences on the farm) and then to Donald MacDonald. The Mrs. Piggle-Wiggle stories were first told to her daughters, Anne and Joan. Ms. MacDonald died in 1958.